Isaac Newton Arnold, John B. Bachelder

Sketch of the Life of Abraham Lincoln

Compiled in most part from the History of Abraham Lincoln, and the

overthrow of slavery

Isaac Newton Arnold, John B. Bachelder

Sketch of the Life of Abraham Lincoln
Compiled in most part from the History of Abraham Lincoln, and the overthrow of slavery

ISBN/EAN: 9783337411763

Printed in Europe, USA, Canada, Australia, Japan

Cover: Foto ©Raphael Reischuk / pixelio.de

More available books at **www.hansebooks.com**

SKETCH OF THE LIFE

.OF

ABRAHAM LINCOLN.

COMPILED IN MOST PART

FROM THE

History of Abraham Lincoln, and the Overthrow of Slavery.

PUBLISHED BY MESSRS. CLARK AND CO., CHICAGO.

BY

ISAAC N. ARNOLD

JOHN B. BACHELDER, PUBLISHER,

59 BEEKMAN STREET, NEW YORK.

1869.

PUBLISHER'S PREFACE.

TIME out of mind, words prefatory have been considered indispensable to the successful publication of a book. This sketch of the LIFE and DEATH of ABRAHAM LINCOLN is intended as an accompaniment to the Historical Painting which has rescued from oblivion, and, with almost perfect fidelity, transmitted to futurity, "THE LAST HOURS OF LINCOLN." In its preparation has been invoked the aid of one who in life was near the heart of MR. LINCOLN, and at death was a witness to that last sad scene, so accurately delineated by the painter's art—the Hon. ISAAC N. ARNOLD. His intimate and social relations with MR. LINCOLN, his unbounded admiration of the goodness and sincerity of the Great Emancipator, renders this invocation eminently appropriate. This sketch contains subject-matter never before made public, presented in the full dress of the author's happiest style.

In confident reliance upon the affection of the people for the great Apostle of Liberty—the Martyr—who in his blood wrote his belief "that all men everywhere should be free," this sketch is submitted.

JANUARY 1, 1860.

CONTENTS.

~~~~~~~~~~

6

CONTENTS.

SKETCH OF THE LIFE

OF

ABRAHAM LINCOLN.

MODERN history furnishes no life more eventful and important, terminated by a death so dramatic, as that of the Martyr President. Poetry and painting, sculpture and eloquence, have all sought to illustrate his career, but the grand epic poem of his life has yet to be written. We are too near him in point of time, fully to comprehend and appreciate his greatness and the vast influence he is to exert upon the world. The storms which marked his tempestuous political career have not yet entirely subsided, and the shock of his fearfully tragic death is still felt; but as the dust and smoke of war pass away, and the mists of prejudice which filled the air during the great conflict clear up, his character will stand out in bolder relief and more perfect outline.

The ablest and most sincere apostle of liberty the world has ever seen was Abraham Lincoln. He was a Christian statesman, with faith in God and man. The two men, whose pre-eminence in American history the world will ever recognize, are Washington and Lincoln. The Republic which the first founded and the latter saved, has already crowned them as models for her children.

Abraham Lincoln was born, February 12th, 1809, in Hardin County, in the Slave State of Kentucky. *

His father Thomas and his grandfather Abraham were born in Rockingham County, Virginia. His ancestors were from Pennsylvania, and were Friends or Quakers. The grandfather after whom he was named, went early to Kentucky, and was murdered by the Indians, while at work upon his farm. The early and fearful conflicts in the dense forests of Kentucky, between the settlers and the Indians, gave to a portion of that beautiful State the name of the "*dark and bloody ground.*" The subject of this sketch was the son, the grandson, and the great grandson of a pioneer. His ancestors had settled on the border, first in Pennsylvania, then in Virginia, and from thence to Kentucky. His grandfather had four sons and two daughters. Thomas the youngest son was the father of Abraham, and his life was a struggle with poverty, a hard-working man with very limited education. He could barely sign his name. In the twenty-eighth year of his age he married Nancy Hanks, a native of Virginia,

---

* When the compiler of the Annals of Congress asked Mr. Lincoln to furnish him with data from which to compile a sketch of his life, the following brief, characteristic statement was given. It contrasts very strikingly with the voluminous biographies furnished by some small great men who have been in Congress:—

"Born, February 12th, 1809, in Hardin County, Kentucky.

"Education defective.

"Profession, a Lawyer.

"Have been a Captain of Volunteers in Black Hawk War.

"Postmaster at a very small office.

"Four times a member of the Illinois Legislature, and was a member of the Lower House of Congress.

                 "Yours, &c.,

                       "A. LINCOLN."

she was one of those plain, dignified matrons, possessing a strong physical organization, and great common sense, with deep religious feeling, and the utmost devotion to her family and children, such as are not unusual in the early settlements of our country. Reared on the frontier, where life was a struggle, she could use the rifle and the implements of agriculture as well as the distaff and spinning-wheel. She was one of those strong, self-reliant characters, yet gentle in manners, often found in the humbler walks of life, fitted as well to command the respect, as the love of all to whom she was known. Abraham had a brother older, and a sister younger than himself, but both died many years before he reached distinction.

In 1816, when he was only eight years old, the family removed to Spenser County, Indiana. The first tool the boy of the backwoods learns to use is the ax. This, young Lincoln, strong and athletic beyond his years, had learned to handle with some effect, even at that early age, and he began from this period to be of important service to his parents in cutting their way to, and building up, a home in the forests.

A feat with the rifle soon after this period shows that he was not unaccustomed to its use: seeing a flock of wild turkeys approaching, the lad seized his father's rifle and succeeded in shooting one through a crack of his father's cabin.

In the autumn of 1818 his mother died. Her death was to her family, and especially her favorite son Abraham, an irreparable loss. Although she died when in his tenth year, she had already deeply impressed upon him those elements of character which were the foundation of his greatness;

perfect truthfulness, inflexible honesty, love of justice and respect for age, and reverence for God. He ever spoke of her with the most touching affection. "All that I am, or hope to be," said he, "I owe to my angel mother."

It was his mother who taught him to read and write; from her he learned to read the Bible, and this book he read and re-read in youth, because he had little else to read, and later in life because he believed it was the word of God, and the best guide of human conduct. It was very rare to find, even among clergymen, any so familiar with it as he, and few could so readily and accurately quote its text.

There is something very affecting in the incident that this boy—whom his mother had found time amidst her weary toil and the hard struggle of her rude life, to teach to write legibly, should find the first occasion of putting his knowledge of the pen to practical use, was in writing a letter to a traveling preacher, imploring him to come and perform religious services over his mother's grave. The preacher, a Mr. Elkin, came, though not immediately, traveling many miles on horseback through the wild forests; and some months after her death the family and neighbors gathered around the tree beneath which they had laid her, to perform the simple, solemn funeral rites. Hymns were sung, prayers said, and an address pronounced over her grave. The impression made upon young Lincoln by his mother was as lasting as life. Love of truth, reverence for religion, perfect integrity, were ever associated in his mind with the tenderest love and respect for her. His father subsequently married Mrs. Sally Johnson, of Kentucky, a widow with three children.

In March, 1830, the family removed to Illinois, and settled in Macon County, near Decatur. Here he assisted his father to build a log-cabin; clear, fence, and plant a few acres of land; and then, being now twenty-one years of age, he asked permission to seek his own fortune. He began by going out to work by the month, breaking up the prairie, splitting and chopping cord wood, and any thing he could find to do. His father not long afterward removed to Coles County, Illinois, where he lived until 1851, dying at the age of seventy-three. He lived to see his son Abraham one of the most distinguished men in the State, and received from him many memorials of his affection and kindness. His son often sent money to his father and other members of his family, and always treated them, however poor and illiterate, with the kindest consideration.

It is clear from his own declarations that he early cherished an ambition, probably under the inspiration of his mother, to rise to a higher position. He had in all less than one year's attendance at school, but his mother having taught him to read and write, with an industry, application, and perseverance untiring, he applied himself to all the means of improvement within his reach. Fortunately, providentially, the Bible has been everywhere and always present in every cabin and home in the land. The influence of this book formed his character; he was able to obtain in addition to the Bible, Esop's Fables, Bunyan's Pilgrim's Progress, Weems' Life of Washington, and Burns' Poems. These constituted nearly all he read before he reached the age of nineteen. Living on the frontier, mingling with the rude, hard-working, honest, and virtuous backwoodsmen, he became expert in the use of every implement of agriculture and woodcraft, and as an ax-man he had no superior.

His days were spent in hard manual labor, and his evenings in study; he grew up free from idleness, and contracted no stain of intemperance, profanity, or vice; he drank no intoxicating liquors, nor did he use tobacco in any form.

There is a tradition that while residing at New Salem, Mr. Lincoln entertained a boy's fancy for a prairie beauty named Ann Rutledge. Mr. Irving, in his life of Washington, says: "Before he (Washington) was fifteen years of age, he had conceived a passion for some unknown beauty, so serious as to disturb his otherwise well-regulated mind, and to make him really unhappy." Some romance has been published in regard to this early attachment of Lincoln, and gossip and imagination have converted a simple, boyish fancy, such as few reach manhood without having passed through, into a "grand passion." It has been produced in a form altogether too dramatic and highly-colored for the truth. The idea that this fancy had any permanent influence upon his life and character is purely imaginary. No man was ever a more devoted and affectionate husband and father than he.

In the spring of 1832 Lincoln volunteered as a private in a company of soldiers raised by the Governor of Illinois, for what is known as the Black Hawk War. He was elected captain of the company, and served during the campaign, but had no opportunity of meeting the enemy.

Soon after his return he was nominated for the State Legislature, and in the precinct in which he resided, out of 284 votes received all but seven. It was while a resident of New Salem that he became a practical surveyor.

Up to this period the life of Lincoln had been one of labor, hardship, and struggle: his shelter had been the log-cabin; his food, the "*corn dodger and common doings,*"* the

---

* The settlers have an expression, "Corn dodger and common doin's," as contradistinguished from "Wheat bread and chicken fixin's."

game of the forests and the prairie, and the products of the farm; his dress, the Kentucky jean and buckskin of the frontier; the tools with which he labored, the ax, the hoe, and the plow. He had made two trips to New Orleans; these and his soldiering in the Black Hawk War showed his fondness for adventure.

Thus far he had been a backwoodsman, a rail-splitter, a flatboatman, a clerk, a captain of volunteers, a surveyor. In 1834 he was elected to the Legislature of Illinois, receiving the highest vote of any one on the ticket. He was re-elected in 1836 (the term being for two years). At this session he met, as a fellow-member, Stephen A. Douglas, then representing Morgan County.

He remained a member of the Legislature for eight years, and then declined being again a candidate.

He was admitted to the bar of the Supreme Court of Illinois in the autumn of 1836, and his name first appears on the roll of attorneys in 1837.

In April of this year he removed to Springfield, and soon after entered into partnership with his friend, John T. Stewart. As a lawyer he early manifested, in a wonderful degree, the power of simplifying and making clear to the common understanding the most difficult and abstruse questions.

The circuit practice—"riding the circuit" it was called —as conducted in Illinois thirty years ago, was admirably adapted to educate, develop, and discipline all there was in a man of intellect and character. Few books could be obtained upon the circuit, and no large libraries for consultation could be found anywhere. A mere case lawyer was a helpless child in the hands of the intellectual giants produced by these circuit-court contests, where novel questions were constantly arising, and must be immediately settled upon principle and analogy.*

A few elementary books, such as Blackstone's and Kent's Commentaries, Chitty's Pleadings, and Starkie's Evidence, could sometimes be found, or an odd volume would be carried along with the scanty wardrobe of the attorney in his saddle-bags. These were studied until the text was as familiar as the alphabet. By such aid as these afforded, and the application of principles, were all the complex questions which arose settled. Thirty years ago it was the practice of the leading members of the bar to follow the judge from county to county. The court-houses were rude log buildings, with slab benches for seats, and the roughest pine tables. In these, when courts were in session, Lincoln could be always found, dressed in Kentucky jean, and always surrounded by a circle of admiring friends— always personally popular with the judges, the lawyers, the jury, and the spectators. His wit and humor, his power of illustration by apt comparison and anecdote, his power to ridicule by ludicrous stories and illustrations, were inexhaustible.

He always aided by his advice and counsel the young members of the bar. No embarrassed tyro in the profession ever sought his assistance in vain, and it was not unusual for him, if his adversary was young and inexperienced, kindly to point out to him formal errors in his pleadings and practice. His manner of conducting jury trials was very effective.

He was familiar, frequently colloquial: at the summer terms of the courts, he would often take off his coat, and leaning carelessly on the rail of the jury box, would

* Vide "History of Abraham Lincoln and the Overthrow of Slavery," p. 76.

single out and address a leading juryman, in a conversational way, and with his invariable candor and fairness would proceed to reason the case. When he was satisfied that he had secured the favorable judgment of the juryman so addressed, he would turn to another, and address him in the same manner, until he was convinced the jury were with him. There were times when aroused by injustice, fraud, or some great wrong or falsehood, when his denunciation was so crushing that the object of it was driven from the court-room.

There was a latent power in him which when aroused was literally overwhelming. This power was sometimes exhibited in political debate, and there were occasions when it utterly paralyzed his opponent. His replies to Douglas, at Springfield and Peoria, in 1858, were illustrations of this power. His examination and cross-examination of witnesses were very happy and effective. He always treated those who were disposed to be truthful with respect.

Mr. Lincoln's professional bearing was so high, he was so courteous and fair that no man ever questioned his truthfulness or his honor. No one who watched him for half an hour in court in an important case ever doubted his ability. He understood human nature well; and read the character of party, jury, witnesses, and attorneys, and knew how to address and influence them. Probably as a jury lawyer, on the right side, he has never had his superior.

Such was Mr. Lincoln at the bar, a fair, honest, able lawyer, on the right side irresistible, on the wrong comparatively weak.

MR. LINCOLN

FROM HIS

RETIREMENT FROM THE ILLINOIS LEGISLATURE

TO HIS

ELECTION TO CONGRESS.

A FRIEND and associate of Mr. Lincoln, speaking of him, as he was in 1840, says: "They mistake greatly who regard him as an uneducated man. In the physical sciences he was remarkably well read. In scientific mechanics, and all inventions and labor-saving machinery, he was thoroughly informed. He was one of the best practical surveyors in the State. He understood the general principles of botany, geology, and astronomy, and had a great treasury of practical useful knowledge."

He continued to acquire knowledge and to grow intellectually until his death, and became one of the most intelligent and best-informed men in public life.

Early in life he became an anti-slavery man, as well from the impulses of his heart as the convictions of his reason. He always had an intense hatred of oppression in every form, and an honest, earnest faith in the common people, and his sympathies were ever with the oppressed. The most conspicuous traits of his character were love of justice and love of truth. It is false, very arrogant, and to those who knew Lincoln in his earlier years, it is very amusing, for any man or set of men to assume to himself or themselves the credit of having inspired him with hatred of slavery. No man was less influenced by others in coming to his conclusions than he; and this was especially true in regard to questions involving right and justice. . His own heart, his own observation, his own clear intellect led him to become an anti-slavery man. Long before he plead the cause of the slave before the American people, he said to a friend,* " It is strange that while our courts decide that a man does not lose his title to his property by its being stolen, but he may reclaim it whenever he can find it, yet if he himself is stolen he instantly loses his right to himself!"

In November, 1842, he was married to Miss Mary Todd, daughter of the Hon. Robert S. Todd, of Kentucky. The mother of Mrs. Lincoln died when she was young. She had sisters living at Springfield, Illinois. Visiting them, she made the acquaintance and won the heart of Mr. Lincoln. They had four children, Robert, Edward (who died in infancy), William, and Thomas. Robert and Thomas survive. William, a beautiful and promising boy, died at Washington, during his father's presidency. Mr. Lincoln was a most fond, tender, and affectionate husband and father. No man was ever more faithful and true in his domestic relations.

* Hon. Jos. Gillespie.

LINCOLN IN CONGRESS.

ON the 6th of December, 1847, Mr. Lincoln took his seat in Congress. Mr. Douglas, who had already run a brilliant career in the lower House of Congress, at this same session took his seat in the Senate. Mr. Lincoln distinguished himself by able speeches upon the Mexican War, upon Internal Improvements, and by one of the most effective campaign speeches of that Congress in favor of the election of General Taylor to the Presidency. He proposed a bill for the abolition of slavery at the National capital. He declined a re-election, and was succeeded by his friend, the eloquent E. D. Baker, who was killed at Ball's Bluff.

In 1852, he lead the electoral ticket of Illinois in favor of General Scott for President. Franklin Pierce was elected, and Mr. Lincoln remained quietly engaged in his professional pursuits until the repeal of the Missouri Compromise in 1854. This event was the beginning of the end of slavery. "It thoroughly roused the people of the Free States to a realization of the progress and encroachments of the slave power, and the necessity of preserving 'the jewel of freedom.'" From that hour the conflict went on between freedom and slavery, first by the ballot, and all the agencies by which public opinion is influenced, and then the slave-holders, seeing that their supremacy was departing, sought by arms to overthrow the government which they could no longer control.

Mr. Lincoln, while a strong opponent of slavery, had up to this time rested in the hope that by peaceful agencies it was in the course of ultimate extinction. But now seeing the vast strides it was making, he became convinced its progress must be arrested or that it would dominate over the republic, and Slavery would become "lawful in all the States." · From this time he gave himself with solemn earnestness to the cause of liberty and his country. He forgot himself in his great cause. He did not seek place, if the great cause could be better ad- vanced by the promotion of another; hence his promotion of the election of Trumbull to the United States Senate.

This unselfish devotion to principle was a great source of his power. Placing himself at the head of those who opposed the extension of, and who believed in the moral wrong of slavery, he entered upon his great mission with a singleness of purpose, an eloquence and power, which made him as the advocate of freedom, the most effective and influential speaker who ever addressed the American people.

He brought to the tremendous struggle between free- dom and slavery physical strength and endurance almost superhuman. Notwithstanding his modesty and the ab- sence of all self-assertion, when we review the conflict from 1854 to 1865, when the struggle closed by the adop- tion of the constitutional amendment abolishing and pro- hibiting slavery forever throughout the republic, it is clear that Lincoln's speeches and writings did more to ac- complish this result than any other agency.

Following the repeal of the Missouri Compromise came the Kansas struggle, and the organization of a great party to resist the encroachments and aggressions of slavery. The people instinctively found the leader of such a party in Lincoln.

Looking over the whole ground, with the sagacity

which marked his far-seeing mind, he saw .that the basis upon which to build were the grand principles of the Declaration of Independence.   This foundation was broad enough to· include old-fashioned Democrats who sympathized with Jefferson in his hatred of slavery; Whigs who had learned their love of liberty from the utterances of the Adamses and Channings, and the earlier speeches of Webster; and anti-slavery men, who recognized Chase and Sumner as their leaders.

He now addressed himself to the work of consolidating out of all these elements a party, the distinctive characteristics of which should be the ·full recognition of the principles of the Declaration of Independence and hostility to the extension of Slavery.   This was the party which in 1856 gave John C. Fremont 114 electoral votes for President, and in 1860, elected Lincoln to the executive chair.

THE LINCOLN AND DOUGLAS DEBATE.

IN the midsummer of 1858, Senator Douglas, whose term approached its close, came home to canvass for re-election. It was in the midst of the Kansas struggle, and although he had broken with the administration of Buchanan, because he resisted the admission of Kansas into the Union, under the fraudulent Lecompton Constitution, and insisted that the people of that State, should enjoy the right by a fair vote, of deciding upon the character of their Constitution,* yet the people of Illinois. did not forget that he was chiefly responsible for the repeal of the Missouri Compromise, and that he had indorsed the Dred Scott decision. On the 17th of June, 1858, the Republican State Convention of Illinois met and by acclamation nominated Mr. Lincoln for the Senate. He was unquestionably more indebted to Douglas for his greatness than to any other person.

In 1856 Lincoln said, "Twenty years ago Judge Douglas and I first became acquainted; we were both young then, he a trifle younger than I. Even then we were both ambitious, I perhaps quite as much as he. With me the race of ambition has proved a flat failure ; with him it has been one of splendid success. His name fills the nation, and it is not unknown in foreign lands. I affect no contempt for the high eminence he has reached ; so reached that the oppressed of my species might have

* That they "should be perfectly free to form and regulate their domestic institutions in their own way."

shared with me in the elevation, I would rather stand
on that eminence than wear the richest crown that ever
pressed a monarch's brow."

Ten years had not gone by, before the modest Lincoln,
then so humbly expressing this noble sentiment, and to
whom at that moment "The race of ambition seemed a
flat failure;" ten years had not passed, ere he had reached
an eminence on which his name filled, not a nation only,
but the world; and he had indeed so reached it, that
the oppressed did share with him in the elevation; and
so far had he passed his then great rival, that the name
of Douglas will be carried down to posterity, chiefly because of its association as a competitor with Lincoln.

But in many particulars Douglas was not an unworthy
competitor.   The contest between these two champions
was perhaps the most remarkable in American history.
They were the acknowledged leaders, each of his party.
Douglas had been a prominent candidate for the presidency,
was well known and personally popular, not only in the
West, but throughout the Union.   Both were men of great
and marked individuality of character.   The immediate
prize was the Senatorship of the great State of Illinois,
and, in the future, the presidency.   The result would large-
ly influence the struggle for freedom in Kansas, and the
question of slavery throughout the Union.   The canvass
attracted the attention of the people everywhere, and the
speeches were reported and published, not only in the
leading papers in the State, but reporters were sent from
most of the large cities, to report the incidents of the
debates, and describe the conflict.

Douglas was at this time unquestionably the leading
debater in the United States Senate. For years he had

been accustomed to meet the great leaders of the nation in Congress, and he had rarely been discomfited. He had contended with Jefferson Davis, and Toombs, and Hunter, and with Chase, and Sumner, and Seward; and his friends claimed that he was the equal, if not the superior, of the ablest. He was fertile in resources, severe in denunciation, familiar with political history, and had participated so many years in Congressional debate, that he handled with readiness and facility all the weapons of political controversy. Of indomitable physical and moral courage, he was certainly among the most formidable men in the nation on the stump. In Illinois, where he had hosts of friends and enthusiastic followers, he possessed a power over the masses unequaled by any other man, a most striking exhibition of which was exhibited in this canvass, in which he held to himself the whole Democratic party of the State. The administration of Buchanan, with all its patronage wielded by the wily and unscrupulous Slidell, and running a separate ticket, was able to detach only 5,000 out of 126,000 votes from him. There was something exciting, something which stirred the blood, in the boldness with which he threw himself into the conflict, and dealt his blows right and left against the Republican party on one side, and the administration of Buchanan, which sought his defeat, on the other.

Two men presenting more striking contrasts, physically, intellectually, and morally, could not anywhere be found. Douglas was a short, sturdy, resolute man, with large head and chest, and short legs; his ability had gained for him the appellation of "The little giant of Illinois."

Lincoln was of the Kentucky type of men, very tall, long-limbed, angular, awkward in gait and attitude, physically a real giant, large-featured, his eyes deep-set under

2

heavy eyebrows, his forehead high and retreating, with
heavy, dark hair.

Their style of speaking, like every thing about them,
was in 'striking contrast. Douglas, skilled by a thousand
conflicts in all the strategy of a face to face encounter,
stepped upon the platform and faced the thousands of
friends and foes around him with an air of conscious
power. There was an air of indomitable pluck, sometimes
something approaching impudence in his manner, when he
looked out on the immense throngs which surged and
struggled before him. Lincoln was modest, but always
self-possessed, with no self-consciousness, his whole mind
evidently absorbed in his great theme, always candid,
truthful, cool, logical, accurate; at times, inspired by his
subject, rising to great dignity and wonderful power. The
impression made by Douglas, upon a stranger who saw
him for the first time on the platform, would be—"that
is a bold, audacious, ready debater, an ugly opponent."
Of Lincoln—"There is a candid, truthful, sincere man, who,
whether right or wrong, believes he is right." Lincoln
argued the side of freedom, with the most thorough conviction that on its triumph depended the fate of the
Republic. An idea of the impression made by Lincoln
in these discussions may be inferred from a remark made
by a plain old Quaker, who, at the close of the Ottawa
debate, said: "Friend, doubtless God *Almighty might* have
made an honester man than Abe Lincoln, but doubtless
he never did." It is curious that the cause of freedom was
plead by a Kentuckian, and that of slavery by a native
of Vermont. Forgetful of the ancestral hatred of slavery
to which he had been born, Douglas had, by marriage,
become a slave-holder. Lincoln had one great advantage

over his antagonist—he was always good-humored; while Douglas sometimes lost his temper, Lincoln never lost his.

The great champions in these debates, and their discussions, have passed into history, and the world has ratified the popular verdict of the day—that Lincoln was the victor. It should be remembered, in justice to the intel·lectual power of Douglas, that Lincoln spoke for liberty, and he was the organ of a new and vigorous party, with a full consciousness of being in the right. Douglas was looking to the presidency as well as the senatorship, and must keep one eye on the slave-holder and the other on the citizens of Illinois.

The debates in the old Continental Congress, and those on the Missouri question of 1820-1, those of Webster and Hayne, and Webster and Calhoun, are all historical; but it may be doubted if either were more important than these of Lincoln and Douglas.

Mr. Lincoln, although his party received a majority of the popular vote was defeated for Senator, because certain Democratic Senators held over from certain Republican districts.

On the 27th of February, 1860, Mr. Lincoln delivered his celebrated Cooper Institute address. Many went to hear the prairie orator, expecting to be entertained with noisy decla·mation, extravagant and verbose, and with plenty of amusing stories. The speech was so dignified, so exact in language and statement, so replete with historical learning, it exhibited such strength and grasp of thought and was so elevated in tone, that the intelligent audience were astonished and delighted. The closing sentence is characteristic, and should never be forgotten by those who advocate the right. " Let us have faith that *right* makes *might*, and in that faith let us to the end dare to do our duty as we understand it."

NOMINATION AND ELECTION AS PRESIDENT.

WHEN the National Convention met at Chicago in the June following, to nominate a candidate for President, while a majority of the delegates were divided among Messrs. Seward, Chase, Cameron, and Bates, Mr. Lincoln was the first choice of a large plurality, and the second choice of all; besides he was personally so popular with the people, his sobriquet of " Honest old Abe," " The Illinois Rail-splitter," satisfied the shrewd men who were studying the best means of securing success, that he was the most available man to head the ticket. These considerations made his nomination a certainty from the beginning.

The nomination was hailed with enthusiasm throughout the Union. Never did a party enter upon a canvass with more zeal and energy. With the usual motives which actuate political parties there were in this canvass mingled a love of country, a devotion to liberty, a keen sense of the wrongs and outrages inflicted upon the Free State men of Kansas, which fired all hearts with enthusiasm. Mr. Lincoln received one hundred and eighty electoral votes, Douglas twelve, Breckinridge seventy-two, and John Bell of Tennessee, thirty-nine. Mr. Lincoln received of the popular vote 1,866,452, a plurality, but not a majority of the whole.

By the election of Mr. Lincoln the executive power of the republic passed from the slave-holders. Mr. Lincoln and the great party who elected him contemplated no interference with slavery in the States. They meant to prevent its further extension, but the slave-holders instinctively felt that with the government in the hands of those who believed slavery morally wrong, the end of slavery was a mere question of time. Rather than yield, the slave aristocracy resolved "to take up the sword," and hence the terrible civil war.

On the 11th of February, 1861, Mr. Lincoln left his quiet happy home at Springfield to enter upon that tempestuous political career which was to lead him through a martyr's grave to a deathless fame among the greatest and noblest patriots and benefactors of mankind. With a dim, mysterious foreshadowing of the future, he uttered to his friends and neighbors who gathered around him to say good-bye, his farewell. He seemed conscious that he might see the place which had been his home for "a quarter of a century, and where his children were born, and where one of them lay buried" no more. Weighed down with the consciousness of the great duties which devolved upon him, greater than those devolving upon any President since Washington, he humbly expressed his reliance upon Divine Providence, and asked his friends to pray that he might receive the assistance of Almighty God." As he journeyed toward the capital, received everywhere with the earnest sympathies of the people, the loyal men of all parties assuring him of their support, his spirits rose, and when he passed the State line of his own State his hopefulness found expression in the words "behind the cloud the sun is shining still." And on he sped through the great Free States of the North. While on his way to the capital the people were everywhere deeply impressed by his modest yet firm reliance upon Providence. He went forth not leaning on his own strength, but resting on Almighty God.

In the early gray of the morning of the 23d of February, 1861, he came in sight of the dome of the Capitol, then filled with traitors plotting his death and the overthrow of the Government. By anticipating the train, by which it had been publicly announced that he would pass through Baltimore, and passing through that city at night he escaped a deeply-laid conspiracy, which would otherwise have anticipated the crime of Booth. None who witnessed will ever forget the scene of his first inauguration.

The veteran Scott had gathered a few soldiers of the Regular Army to preserve order and security; many Northern citizens thronged the streets, few of them conscious of the volcano of treason and murder seething beneath them. The departments and public offices were full of plotting traitors. Many of the rebel generals held commissions under the Government they were about to desert and betray The ceremony of inauguration is always imposing; on this occasion it was especially so. Buchanan, sad, dejected, bowed with a seeming consciousness of duties unperformed, rode with the President-elect to the Capitol.

There were gathered the Justices of the Supreme Court, both Houses of Congress, the representatives of foreign nations, and a vast concourse of citizens from all sections of the Union. There were Chase, and Seward, and Sumner, and Breckinridge, and Douglas, who was near the President, and was observed eagerly looking over the crowd, not unconscious of the personal danger of his great and successful rival. Mr. Lincoln was so absorbed with the gravity of the occasion and the condition of his country, that he utterly forgot himself, and there was observed a dignity, which sprung from a mind entirely engrossed with public duties.

He was perfectly cool, and stepping to the eastern colonnade of the Capitol, that voice, which had been often heard by tens of thousands on the prairies of the West, now read in clear and ringing tones his inaugural. On the threshold of war, he made a last appeal for peace. He declared his fixed resolve, firm as the everlasting rocks: "*I shall take care that the laws of the Union be faithfully executed in every State.*"

Yet his great, kind heart yearned for peace, and as he approached the close, his voice faltered with emotion. "I am loath to close," said he; "we are *not* enemies, but friends; we must not be enemies. Though passion may have strained, it must not break the bonds of affection. The mystic cords of memory, stretching from every battle-field and patriot's grave, to every living heart and hearthstone over all this broad land, will yet swell with the chorus of the Union, when again touched, as surely they will be, by the better angels of our nature."

Alas! these appeals for peace were received by those to whom they were addressed with coarse ribaldry, with sneers and jeers, and all the savage and barbarous passions which riot in blood. Lincoln was somewhat slow to learn that it was to force only—stern, unflinching force—that treason would yield.

And now opened that terrible civil war which has no parallel in history. Space will not permit me to follow the President through those long and terrible days of victory and defeat, to final triumph. Through all, Lincoln was firm, constant, hopeful, sagacious, wise, confiding always in God, and in the people.

THE THIRTY-SEVENTH CONGRESS.

THE special session of the Thirty-seventh Congress met on the 4th of July, 1861, agreeably to the call of the President. Many vacant chairs in the National Council impressed the spectator with the magnitude of the impending struggle. The old chiefs of the slave party were nearly all absent, some of them as members of a rebel government at Richmond, others in arms against their country. The President calmly, clearly, sadly reviewed the facts which compelled him to call into action the *war powers* of the Government, and constrained him, as the Chief Magistrate, "*to accept war.*" He asked Congress to confer upon him the power to make the war short and decisive. He asked for 400,000 men and 400 millions of money. With hearty appreciation of the fidelity of the common people, he proudly points to the fact that, while large numbers of the officers of the Army and Navy had been guilty of the infamous crime of desertion, "not one common soldier or sailor is known to have deserted his flag."

Congress responded promptly to this call, voting 500,000 men and 500 millions of dollars to suppress the rebellion. From the beginning of the contest, the slaves flocked to the Union army as a place of security from their masters. They seemed to feel instinctively that freedom was to be found within its picket-lines and under the folds of its flag. They were ready to act as guides, as servants, to work, dig, and to fight for their liberty. And yet early in the war some officers permitted masters and agents to follow the blacks into the Union lines and carry away fugitive slaves. This action was rebuked by a resolution of Congress. At this session a law was passed giving freedom to all slaves employed in aiding the rebellion. In October, 1861, the military was authorized by the Secretary of War to avail itself of the services of "fugitives from labor," in such way as might be most beneficial to the service.

The regular session of Congress assembled on the 2d of December, 1861. Great armies confronted each other in the field; and great conflicts were going on in the public mind, but the way to victory through emancipation was not yet clearly opened. The President was feeling his way, watching the progress of public opinion; striving to secure to the Union the Border States of Maryland, Kentucky, and Missouri. On the subject of Emancipation, he said in his message: ." the Union must be preserved, and all *indispensable means* must be used," but he wisely waited until the public sentiment should consolidate, and all other means of maintaining the integrity of the nation should have been exhausted. During this session the way was prepared for the great edict of Emancipation; Slavery was abolished at the National Capital, prohibited forever in all the Territories, the slaves of rebels declared free, and the Government authorized to employ slaves as soldiers, and every person in the military or naval service of the Republic prohibited from aiding in the arrest of any fugitive slave. These measures were all urged by the personal and political friends of the President, and became laws with his sanction and hearty assent. They prepared the way for the final overthrow of slavery.

THE EMANCIPATION PROCLAMATION.

In April, 1862, it was known at Washington that the President was considering the subject of emancipating the slaves as a war measure. The Border States selected their ablest man, the venerable John J. Crittenden, from Mr. Lincoln's native State, to make a public appeal to him to stay his hand. The eloquent Kentuckian discharged the part assigned him well. Never shall I forget the scene when, with great emotion before Congress he said, that although he had voted against and opposed Mr. Lincoln, he had been won to his side. "*And now,*" said he, " there is a niche near to Washington which should be occupied by him who shall save his country. Mr. Lincoln has a mighty destiny ! * * * He is no coward, he may be President *of all the people* and fill that niche, but if he chooses to be in these times a mere sectarian and party man, that place will be reserved for some future and better patriot." " It is in his power to occupy a place next to Washington, the *founder* and *preserver* side by side." It was understood the Border State men everywhere were ready to crown him the peer of Washington if he would not touch slavery

It was OWEN LOVEJOY, the early abolitionist, who made an instantaneous, impromptu reply, a reply the eloquence of which thrilled Congress and the country, and is in my judgment among the finest specimens of American eloquence.

Said he, "Let Abraham Lincoln make himself, as I

trust he will, the Emancipator, the liberator of a race, and his name shall not only be enrolled in this earthly temple, but it will be traced on the living stones of that Temple, which rears itself amidst the thrones of Heaven." Alluding to what Crittenden had said, he added, "There is a niche for Abraham Lincoln in Freedom's holy fane. In that niche he shall stand proudly, gloriously, with shattered fetters, and broken chains and slave-whips beneath his feet. * * This is a fame worth living for; ay, more, it is a fame worth *dying* for, even though (said he with prophetic prescience) that death led through the blood of Gethsemane and the agony of the accursed tree."

These two speeches were read to Mr. Lincoln in his library at the White House, a room to which he sometimes retired. He was moved by the picture which Lovejoy drew. The tremendous responsibilities growing out of the slavery question, how he ought to treat those sons of "unrequited toil," were questions sinking deeper and deeper into his heart. With a purpose firmly to follow the path of duty, as God should give him to see his duty, he earnestly sought the divine guidance.

Speaking afterward of Emancipation, Mr. Lincoln said: "When, in March, May, and July, 1862, I made earnest and successive appeals to the Border States to favor compensated emancipation, I believed the indispensable necessity for military emancipation and arming the blacks would come, unless averted by that measure. They declined the proposition and I was in my best judgment driven to the alternative of either surrendering the Union or issuing the Emancipation Proclamation." *

Before issuing the proclamation, he had appealed to the

* See Letter of the President to A. G. Hodges, dated April 4, 1864.

Border States to adopt gradual emancipation. His appeal is one of the most earnest and eloquent papers in all history. "Our country," said he, "is in great peril, demanding the loftiest views and boldest action to bring a speedy relief; once relieved, its form of government is saved to the world, its beloved history and cherished memories are vindicated, and its future fully assured and rendered inconceivably grand."

The appeal was received by some with apathy, by others with caviling and opposition, and was followed by action on the part of none. Meanwhile his friends urged emancipation. They declared there could be no permanent peace while slavery lived. "Seize," cried they, "the thunderbolt of Liberty, and shatter Slavery to atoms, and then the Republic will live." After the great battle of Antietam, the President called his cabinet together, and announced to them that "*in obedience to a solemn vow to God*," he was about to issue the edict of Freedom.

The proclamation came, modestly, sublimely, reverently the great act was done. "Sincerely believing it to be an act of justice, warranted by the Constitution, upon military necessity, he invoked upon it the considerate judgment of mankind and the gracious favor of Almighty God."

On the first of January, 1863, the Executive mansion, as is usual on New Year's Day, was crowded with the officials, foreign and domestic, of the National Capital; the men of mark of the army and navy and from civil life crowded around the care-worn President, to express their kind wishes for him personally, and their prayers for the future of the country.

During the reception, after he had been shaking hands with hundreds, a secretary hastily entered and told him the

Proclamation (the final proclamation) was ready for his signature. Leaving the crowd, he went to his office, taking up a pen, attempting to write, and was astonished to find he could not control the muscles of his hand and arm sufficiently to write his name. He said to me, "I paused, and a feeling of superstition, a sense of the vast responsibility of the act, came over me; then, remembering that my arm had been well-nigh paralyzed by two hours' of hand-shaking, I smiled at my superstitious feeling, and wrote my name."

This Proclamation, the Declaration of Independence, and *Magna Charta*, these be great landmarks, each indicating an advance to a higher and more Christian civilization. Upon these will the historian linger, as the stepping-stones toward a higher plane of existence. From this time the war meant *universal liberty*. When, in June, 1858, at his home in Springfield, Lincoln startled the country by the announcement, "this nation can not endure half *slave*, and *half free*," and when he concluded that remarkable speech by declaring, with uplifted eye and the inspired voice of a prophet, "we shall not fail if we stand firm, *we shall not fail*, wise councils may accelerate or mistakes delay, but sooner or later the victory is sure to come," he looked to years of peaceful controversy and final triumph through the ballot-box. He anticipated no war, and he did not foresee, unless in those mysterious, dim shadows, which sometimes startle by half revealing the future, his own elevation to the presidency; he little dreamed that he was to be the instrument in the hands of God to speak those words which should emancipate a race and free his country!

I have not space to follow the movements of the armies; the long, sad campaigns of the grand army of the Potomac under McClellan, Pope, Burnside, Hooker, Meade; nor the varying fortunes of war in the great Valley of the Mississippi under Freemont, and Halleck, and Buell. Armies had not only to be organized, but educated and trained, and especially did the President have to search for and find those fitted for high command.

Ultimately he found such and placed them at the head of the armies. Up to 1863, there had been vast expenditures of blood and treasure, and, although great successes had been achieved and progress made, yet there had been so many dis-asters and grievous failures, that the hopes of the insurgents of final success were still confident. With all the great vic-tories in the South, and Southwest, by land and on the sea, the Mississippi was still closed. The President opened the campaign of 1863 with the determination of accomplishing two great objects, first to get control of and open the Missis-sippi; second to destroy the army of Virginia under Lee, and sieze upon the rebel capital. By the capture of Vicksburg, and the fall of Port Hudson, the first and primary object of the campaign was realized.

"The 'Father of Waters' again went unvexed to the sea. Thanks to the great Northwest for it, nor yet wholly to them. Three hundred miles up they met New England, Empire, Keystone, and Jersey, hewing their way right and left. The army South, too, in more colors than one, lent a helping hand."* While the gallant armies of the West were achieving these victories, operations in the East were crowned by the decisively important triumph at Gettysburg. Let us pass over the scenes of conflict, on the sea and on the land, at the East and at the West, and come to that touching incident in the life of Lincoln, the consecration of the battle-field of Gettys-burg as a National cemetery.

---

* See letter of Mr. Lincoln to State Convention of Illinois.

GETTYSBURG.

Here, late in the autumn of that year of battles, a portion of that battle-ground was to be consecrated as the last resting-place of those who there gave their lives that the Republic might live.

There were gathered there the President, his Cabinet, members of Congress, Governors of States, and a vast and brilliant assemblage of officers, soldiers, and citizens, with solemn and impressive ceremonies to consecrate the earth to its pious purpose. New England's most distinguished orator and scholar was selected to pronounce the oration. The address of Everett was worthy of the occasion. When the elaborate oration was finished, the tall, homely form of Lincoln arose; simple, rude, majestic, slowly he stepped to the front of the stage, drew from his pocket a manuscript, and commenced reading that wonderful address, which an English scholar and statesman has pronounced the finest in the English language. The polished periods of Everett had fallen somewhat coldly upon the ear, but Lincoln had not finished the first sentence before the magnetic influence of a grand idea eloquently uttered by a sympathetic nature, pervaded the vast assemblage. He said:—

" Fourscore and seven years ago, our fathers brought forth on this continent a new nation, conceived in Liberty, and dedicated to the proposition that all men are created equal.

" Now we are engaged in a great civil war, testing whether that nation, or any nation, so conceived and so dedicated, can long endure. We are met on a great battle-field of that war. We have come to dedicate a portion of that field as a final resting-place for those who here gave their lives that that nation might live. It is altogether fitting and proper that we should do this.

"But, in a larger sense, we can not dedicate—we can not consecrate—we can not hallow this ground. The brave men, living and dead, who struggled here, have consecrated it far above our poor power to add or detract. The world will little note, nor long remember what we *say* here, but it can never forget what they *did* here. It is for us, the living, rather, to be dedicated here to the unfinished work which they who fought here have thus far so nobly advanced.

"It is, rather, for us to be here dedicated to the great task remaining before us, that from these honored dead we take increased devotion to that cause for which they gave the last full measure of devotion, that we here highly resolve that these dead shall not have died in vain: that this nation, under God, shall have a new birth of freedom: and that government of the people, by the people, and for the people, shall not perish from the earth."

He was so absorbed with the heroic sacrifices of the soldiers as to be utterly unconscious that he was *the great actor* in the drama, and that his simple words would live as long as the memory of the heroism he there commemorated.

Closing his brief address amidst the deepest emotions of the crowd, he turned to Everett and congratulated him upon his success. "Ah, Mr. Lincoln," said the orator, "I would gladly exchange my hundred pages for your twenty lines."

1864.

On the first of January, 1864, Mr. Lincoln received his friends as was usual on New Year's day, and the improved prospects of the country, made it a day of congratulation.

The decisive victories East and West enlivened and made buoyant and hopeful the spirits of all. One of the most devoted friends of Mr. Lincoln calling upon him, after exchanging congratulations over the progress of the Union armies during the past year, said :—

"I hope, Mr. President, one year from to-day, I may have the pleasure of congratulating you on the consummation of three events which seem now very probable."

"What are they?" said Mr. Lincoln.

"First, That the rebellion may be completely crushed. Second, That slavery may be entirely destroyed, and prohibited forever throughout the Union. Third, That Abraham Lincoln may have been triumphantly re-elected President of the United States."

"I would be very glad," said Mr. Lincoln, with a twinkle in his eye, "to compromise, by securing the success of the first two propositions."

LIEUTENANT-GENERAL GRANT.

On the 22d of February, 1864, President Lincoln nominated General U. S. Grant as Lieutenant-General of all the armies of the United States, and on the 9th of March, at the White House, he, in person, presented the victorious General with his commission, and sent him forth to consummate with the armies of the East, his world-renowned successes at the West. Then followed the memorable campaign of 1864-5. Sherman's brilliant Atlanta campaign; Sheridan's glorious career in the Valley of the Shenandoah; Thomas's victories in Tennessee, the triumph at Look-out Mountain; Sherman's "Grand march to the sea," the fall of

3

Mobile, the capture of Fort Fisher, and Wilmington, indicating the near approach of peace through war. In the midst of these successes, Mr. Lincoln was triumphantly re-elected, the people thereby stamping upon his administration their grateful approval. At the session of Congress, of 1864–5, he urged the adoption of an amendment of the Constitution abolishing and prohibiting slavery forever throughout the Republic, thereby consummating his own great work of Emancipation.

CONSTITUTIONAL AMENDMENT ABOLISHING SLAVERY.

As the great leader in the overthrow of slavery, he had seen his action sanctioned by an emphatic majority of the people, and now the constitutional majority of two-thirds of both branches of Congress had voted to submit to the States this amendment of the organic law.

Illinois, the home of Lincoln, as was fit, took the lead in ratifying this amendment, and other States rapidly followed, until more than the requisite number was obtained, and the amendment adopted. Meanwhile, military successes continued, until the victory over slavery and rebellion was won.

LINCOLN'S SECOND INAUGURATION.

It was known, by a dispatch received at the Capitol at midnight, on the 3d of March, 1865, that Lee had sought an interview with Grant, to arrange terms of surrender. On the next day Lincoln again stood on the eastern colonnade of the Capitol, again to swear fidelity to the Republic, her Constitution, and laws; but, how changed the scene form his first inauguration. No traitors now occupied high places under the Government. Crowds of citizens and soldiers who would have died for their beloved Chief Magistrate now thronged the area. Liberty loyalty, and victory had crowned the eagles of our armies. No conspirators were now mingling in the crowd, unless perchance the assassin Booth might have been lurking there. Many patriots and statesmen were in their graves. Douglas was dead, and Ellsworth, and Baker, and McPherson, and Reynolds, and Wadsworth, and a host of martyrs, had given their lives that liberty and the Republic might triumph. It was a very touching spectacle to see the long lines of invalid and wounded soldiers, from the great hospitals about Washington, some on crutches, some who had lost an arm, many pale from unhealed wounds, who gathered to witness the scene. As Lincoln ascended the platform, and his tall form, towering above all his associates, was recognized, cheers and shouts of welcome filled the air, and not until he raised his arm motioning for silence, could the acclamations be hushed. He paused a moment, looked over the scene, and still hesitated. What thronging memories passed through his mind! Here, four years before, he had stood pleading, oh, how earnestly, for *peace*. But, even while he pleaded, the rebels took up the sword, and he was forced to "*accept war*."

Now four long, bloody, weary years of devastating war had passed, and those who made the war were everywhere discomfited, and being overthrown. That barbarous institution which had caused the war, had been destroyed, and the dawn of peace already brightened the sky. Such the scene, and such the circumstances under which Lincoln pronounced his second Inaugural, a speech which has no parallel since Christ's Sermon on the Mount.

Who shall say that I am irreverent when I declare, that

the passage, " Fondly do we hope, fervently do we pray that this *mighty scourge* of war *may speedily pass away !* yet, if God wills that it continue until all the wealth piled by the bondsmen's two hundred and fifty years of unrequited toil shall be sunk, and every drop of blood drawn by the lash, shall be paid by another drawn by the sword, as was said three thousand years ago, so it must be said now, that the judgments of the Lord are true and righteous altogether," could only have been inspired by that *Holy Book*, which daily he read, and from which he ever sought guidance ?

Where, but from the teachings of Christ, could he have learned that charity in which he so unconsciously described his own moral nature, " *With malice toward none, with charity for all*, with firmness in the right, as God gives us to see the right, let us finish the work we are in, *to bind up the nation's wounds*, to care for him who hath borne the battle, and for his widow and his orphans, to do all which may achieve a just and lasting peace, among ourselves and among all nations."

END OF THE WAR.

And now Mr. Lincoln gave his whole attention to the movements of the armies, which, as he confidently hoped, were on the eve of final and complete triumph. On the 27th of March he visited the head-quarters of General Grant, at City Point, to concert with his most trusted military chiefs the final movements against Lee, and Johnston. Grant was still at bay before Petersburg. Sherman with his veterans, after occupying Georgia and South Carolina, had reached Goldsboro', North Carolina, on his victorious march north. It was the hope and purpose of the two great leaders, whose generous friendship for each other made them ever like brothers, now and there to crush the armies of Lee and Johnston, and finish the "job."

An artist has worthily painted the scene of the meeting of Lincoln and his cabinet, when he first announced and read to them his proclamation of Emancipation.   Another artist is now recording for the American people the scene of this memorable meeting of the President and the Generals, which took place in the cabin of the steamer "River Queen," lying at the dock in the James River. Three men more unlike personally and mentally, and yet of more distinguished ability, have rarely been called together. Although so entirely unlike, each was a type of American character, and all had peculiarities not only American, but Western.

Lincoln's towering form had acquired dignity by his great deeds, and the great ideas to which he had given expression.   His rugged features, lately so deeply fur-rowed with care and responsibility, were now radiant with hope and confidence.   He met the two great leaders with grateful cordiality ; with clear intelligence he grasped the military situation, and listened with eager confidence to their details of the final moves which should close this terrible game of war.

Contrasting, with the giant-like stature of Lincoln, was the short, sturdy, resolute form of the hero of Fort Donel-son and Vicksburg, so firm and iron-like, every feature of his face and every attitude and movement so quiet, yet all expressive of inflexible will and never faltering determi-nation, "to fight it out on this line."

There, too, was Sherman, with his broad intellectual

forehead, his restless eye, his nervous energy, his sharply
outlined features bronzed by that magnificent campaign
from Chattanooga to Atlanta and from Atlanta to the Sea,
and now fresh from the conquest of Georgia and South
Carolina. On the eve of final triumph, Lincoln, with
characteristic humanity deplored the necessity which all
realized, of one more hard and deadly battle. They
separated, Sherman hastening to his post, and Grant commenced those brilliant movements which in ten days ended
the war. Now followed in rapid succession the fall of
Richmond, the surrender of Lee, the capitulation of Johnston and his army, the capture of Jefferson Davis, and
the final overthrow of the rebellion.

The Union troops, on the morning of the 4th of April,
entered the rebel capital. Among the exulting columns which
followed the eagles of the Republic, were some regiments of
negro soldiers, who marched through the streets of Richmond
singing their favorite song of "John Brown's soul is marching
on."

On the day of its capture, President Lincoln, with Admiral
Porter, visited Richmond. Leading his youngest son, a lad,
by the hand, he walked from the James River landing to the
house just vacated by the rebel President. From the time
of the issuing of his proclamation to this, his triumphant
entry into the rebel capital, he had been ever ready and
anxious for peace. To all the world he had proclaimed, what
he said so emphatically to the rebel emissaries at Hampton
Roads. "There are just two indispensable conditions of
peace, national unity, and national liberty." "The national
authority must be restored through all the States, and I will
never recede.from my position on the slavery question." He
would never violate the national faith, and now God had

crowned his efforts with complete success. He entered Richmond as a conqueror, but as its preserver he issued no decree of proscription or confiscation, and to all the South his policy was, "with malice toward none, with charity for all, with firmness in the right as God gave him to see the right, he sought to finish the work, and do all which should achieve and cherish a just and lasting peace."

On the 9th of April he returned to Washington, and had scarcely arrived at the White House before the news of the surrender of Lee and all his army reached him. No language can adequately describe the joy and gratitude which filled the hearts of the President and the people.

And here, before the attempt is made to sketch the darkest and most dastardly crime in all our annals, let us pause for one moment to mention that last review on the 22d and 23d of May, of these victorious citizen soldiers, who had come at the call of the President, and who, their work being done, were now to return again to their homes scattered throughout the country they had saved.

These bronzed and scarred veterans who had survived the battle-fields of four years of active war, whose field of operations had been a continent, the brave men who had marched and fought their way from New England and the Northwest, to New Orleans and Charleston; those who had withstood and repelled the terrific charges of the rebels at Gettysburg; those who had fought beneath and above the clouds at Lookout Mountain; who had taken Fort Donelson, Vicksburg, Atlanta, New Orleans, Savannah, Mobile, Petersburg, and Richmond; the triumphal entry of these heroes into the National Capital of the Republic which they had saved and redeemed, was deeply impressive. Triumphal arches, garlands, wreaths of flowers, evergreens, marked their pathway. Acting President and Cabinet, Governors and Senators, ladies, children, citizens, all united to express the nation's gratitude to those by whose heroism it had been saved.

But there was one great shadow over the otherwise bril-liant spectacle. Lincoln, their great-hearted chief, he whom all loved fondly to call their "Father Abraham;" he whose heart had been ever with them in camp, and on the march, in the storm of battle, and in the hospital; he had been mur-dered, stung to death, by the fang of the expiring serpent which these soldiers had crushed. There were many thou-sands of these gallant men in Blue, as they filed past the White House, whose weather-beaten faces were wet with tears of manly grief. How gladly, joyfully would they have given their lives to have saved his.

LAST DAYS OF LINCOLN.

It has been already stated that Mr. Lincoln returned to the Capital on the 9th of April; from that day until the 14th was a scene of continued rejoicing, gratulation, and thanks-giving to Almighty God who had given to us the victory. In every city, town, village, and school district, bells rang, salutes were fired, and the Union flag, now worshiped more than ever by every loyal heart, waved from every home. The President was full of hope and happiness. The clouds were breaking away, and his genial, kindly nature was revolving plans of reconciliation and peace. How could he now bind up the wounds of his country and obliterate the scars of the war, and restore friendship and good feeling to every section? These considerations occupied his thoughts: there was no bit-terness, no desire for revenge. On the morning of the 14th, Robert Lincoln, just returned from the army, where, on the staff of General Grant, he had witnessed the surrender of Lee, breakfasted with his father, and the happy hour was passed in listening to details of that event. The day was occupied, first, with an interview with Speaker Colfax, then exchanging congratulations with a party of old Illinois friends, then a cabinet meeting, attended by Gen. Grant, at which all remarked his hopeful, joyous spirit, and all bear testimony that in this hour of triumph, he had no thought of vengeance, but his mind was revolving the best means of bringing back to sincere loyalty, those who had been making war upon his country. He then drove out with Mrs. Lincoln alone, and during the drive he dwelt upon the happy prospect now before them, and contrasting the gloomy and distracting days of the war with the peaceful ones now in anticipation, and looking beyond the term of his Presidency, he, in imagination, saw the time when he should return again to his prairie home, meet his old friends, and resume his old mode of life. In fancy, he was again in his old law library, and before the courts: with these were mingled visions of a prairie farm, and once more the plow and the ax should become familiar to his hand. Such were some of the incidents and fancies of the last day of the life of Abraham Lincoln.

THE ASSASSINATION.

From the time of the election of Mr. Lincoln to the Presidency, many threats, public and private, were made of his assassination. An attempt to murder him would undoubtedly have been made, in February, 1861, on his passage through Baltimore, had not the plot been discovered, and the time of his passage been anticipated. From the day of his inauguration, he began to recieve letters threatening assassination. He said: "The first one or two made me uncomfortable, but," said he, smiling, "there is nothing like getting *used* to things." He was constitutionally fearless, and came to consider these letters as idle threats, meant only to annoy him, and it was very difficult for his friends to induce him to resort to any precautions.

It was announced through the press that on the evening of the 14th of April, Mr. Lincoln and General Grant would attend Ford's Theater. The General did not attend, but Mr. Lincoln, being unwilling to disappoint the public expectation, accompanied by Mrs. Lincoln, Miss. Harris, and Major Rathbone, was induced to go. The writer met him on the portico of the White House just as he was about to enter his carriage, exchanged greetings, with him, and will never forget the radiant, happy expression of his countenance, and the kind, genial tones of his voice, as we parted *for the night* as we then thought—*forever* in this world, as it resulted.

The President was received, as he always was, by acclamations. When he reached the door of his box, he turned, and smiled, and bowed in acknowledgment of the hearty greeting which welcomed him, and then followed Mrs. Lincoln into the box. This was at the right hand of the stage. In the corner nearest the stage sat Miss Harris, next her Mrs. Lincoln. Mr. Lincoln sat nearest the entrance, Major Rathbone being seated on a sofa, in the back part of the box. The theater, and especially the box occupied by the President's party, was most beautifully draped with the national colors. While the play was in progress, John Wilkes Booth visited the theater behind the scenes, left a horse ready saddled in the alley behind the building, leaving a door opening to this alley ready for his escape.

In the midst of the play, at the hour of 10.30, a pistol shot, sharp and clear, is heard ! a man with a bloody dagger in his hand leaps from the President's box to the stage exclaiming, " *Sic semper tyrannis*," " the South is avenged." As the assassin struck the stage, the spur on his boot having caught in the folds of the flag, he fell to his knee. Instantly rising, he brandished his dagger, darted across the stage, out of the door he had left open, mounted his horse and galloped away. The audience, startled and stupefied with horror, were for a few seconds spell-bound. Some one cries out in the crowd, " *John Wilkes Booth !*" This man, an actor, familiar with the locality, after arranging for his escape, had passed round to the front of the theater, entered, passed in to the President's box, entered at the open and unguarded door, and stealing up behind the President, who was intent upon the play, placed his pistol near the back of the head of Mr. Lincoln, and fired. The ball penetrated the brain, and the President fell upon his face mortally wounded, unconscious and speechless from the first. Major Rathbone had attempted to seize Booth as he rushed past toward the stage, and received from the assassin a severe cut in the arm.

No words can describe the anguish and horror of Mrs. Lincoln. The scene was heart-rending ; she prayed for death to relieve her suffering. The insensible form of the President was removed across the street to the house of a Mr. Peterson. Robert Lincoln soon reached the scene, and the members of the cabinet and personal friends crowded around the place of the fearful tragedy. And there the strong constitution of Mr. Lincoln struggled with death, until twenty-two minutes past seven the next morning, when his heart ceased to beat. The scene during that long fearful night of woe, at the house of Peterson, beggars description.

News of the appalling deed spread through the city, and it was found necessary to restrain the anxious, weeping people by a double guard around the house. The surgeons from the first examination of the wound, pronounced it mortal; and the shock and the agony of that terrible night to Mrs. Lincoln was enough to distract the reason, and break the heart of the most self-controlled. Robert Lincoln sought, by manly self-mastery to control his own grief and soothe his mother, and aid her to sustain her overwhelming sorrow.

When at last, the noble heart ceased to beat, the Rev. Dr. Gurley, in the presence of the family, the household, and those friends of the President who were present, knelt down, and touchingly prayed the Almighty Father, to aid and strengthen the family and friends to bear their terrible sorrow.

I will not attempt with feeble pen to sketch the scenes of that terrible night; I leave that for the pencil of the artist!

As has been said, the name of the assassin was John Wilkes Booth! He was shot by Boston Corbett, a soldier on the 21st of April.

ATTEMPTED ASSASSINATION OF SECRETARY SEWARD.

On the same night of the assassination of the President, an accomplice of Booth attempted to murder Mr. Seward, the Secretary of State, in his own house, while confined to his bed from severe injuries received by being thrown from his carriage. He was terribly mangled; and his life was saved by the heroic efforts of his sons and daughter and a nurse, whose name was Robinson. Some of the accomplices of Booth were arrested, tried, convicted, and hung ; but all were the mere tools and instruments of the Conspirators. Mystery and darkness yet hang over the chief instigators of this most cowardly murder : none can say whether the chief conspirators will ever, in this world, be dragged to light and punishment.

The terrible news of the death of Lincoln was, on the morning of the 15th, borne by telegraph to every portion of the Republic. Coming, as it did, in the midst of universal joy, no language can picture the horror and grief of the people on its reception. A whole nation wept. Persons who had not heard the news, coming into crowded cities, were struck with the strange aspect of the people. All business was suspended ; gloom, sadness, grief, sat upon every face. The flag, which had everywhere, from every spire and masthead, roof, and tree, and public building, been floating in glorious triumph, was now lowered ; and, as the hours of that dreary 15th of April passed on, the people, by common impulse, each family by itself, commenced draping their houses and public buildings in mourning, and before night the whole nation was shrouded in black.

There were no classes of people in the Republic whose grief was more demonstrative than that of the soldiers and the freedmen. The vast armies, not yet disbanded, looked upon Lincoln as their father. They knew his heart had followed them in all their campaigns and marches and battles. Grief and vengeance filled their hearts. But the poor negroes everywhere wept and sobbed over a loss which they instinctively felt was to them irreparable. On the Sunday following his death, the whole people gathered to their places of public worship, and mingled their tears together over a bereavement which every one felt like the loss of a father or a brother. The remains of the President were taken to the White House. On the 17th, on Monday, a meeting of the members of Congress then in Washington, was held at the Capitol, to make arrangements for the funeral. This meeting named a committee of one member from each State and Territory, and the whole Congressional delegation from Illinois, as a Congressional Committee to attend the remains of Mr. Lincoln to their final resting-place in Illinois. Senator Sumner and others desired that his body should be placed under the dome of the Capitol at Washington. It was stated that a vault had been prepared there for the remains of Washington, but had never been used, because the Washington family and Virginia desired them to remain in the family vault at Mount Vernon. It was said it would be peculiarly appropriate for the remains of Lincoln to be deposited under the dome of the Capitol of the Republic he had saved and redeemed.

The funeral took place on Wednesday, the 19th. The services were held in the East Room of the Executive Mansion. It was a bright, genial day—typical of the kind and genial nature of him whom a nation was so deeply mourning.

After the sad ceremonies at the National Capital, the remains of the President and of his beloved son Willie, who died at the White House during his presidency, were placed on a funeral car, and started on its long pilgrimage to his old home in Illinois, and it was arranged that the train should take nearly the same route as that by which he had come from Springfield to Washington in assuming the Executive Chair.

And now the people of every State, city, town, and hamlet, came with uncovered heads, with streaming eyes, with their offerings of wreaths and flowers, to witness the passing train. It is impossible to describe the scenes. Minute-guns, the tolling of bells, music, requiems, dirges, military and civic displays, draped flags, black covering every public building and private house, everywhere indicated the pious desire of the people to do honor to the dead: two thousand miles, along which every house was draped in black, and from which, everywhere, hung the national colors in mourning. The funeral ceremonies at Baltimore were peculiarly impress-ive: nowhere were the manifestations of grief more uni-versal; but the sorrow of the negroes, who thronged the streets in thousands, and hung like a dark fringe upon the long procession, was especially impressive. Their coarse, homely features were convulsed with a grief which they could not control; their emotional natures, excited by the scene, and by each other, until sobs and cries and tears, rolling down their black faces, told how deeply they felt their loss. When the remains reached Philadelphia, a half million of people were in the streets, to do honor to all that was left of him, who, in old Independence Hall, four years before, had de-clared that he would sooner die, sooner be assassinated, than give up the principles of the Declaration of Independence. He *had* been assassinated because he would *not* give them up. All felt, when the remains were placed in that historic room, surrounded by the memories of the great men of the Past, whose portraits from the walls looked down upon the scene, that a peer of the best and greatest of the revolutionary wor-thies was now added to the list of those who had served the Republic.

Through New Jersey, New York, Ohio, Indiana, to Illinois, all the people followed the funeral train as mourners, but when the remains reached his own State, where he had been personally known to every one, where the people had all heard him on the stump and in court, every family mourned him as a father and a brother. The train reached Springfield on the.3d of May; and the corpse was taken to Oak Ridge Cemetery, and there, among his old friends and neighbors, his clients, and constituents, surrounded by representatives from the Army and Navy, with delegations from every State, with all the people,-the world for his mourners—was he buried.

PERSONAL SKETCHES OF LINCOLN.*

In the remaining pages, I shall attempt to give a word-picture of Mr. Lincoln, his person, his moral and intellectual characteristics, and some personal recollections, so as to aid the reader, as far as I may be able, in forming an ideal of the man.

Physically, he was a tall, spare man, six feet and four inches in height. He stooped, leaning forward as he walked. He was very athletic, with long, sinewy arms, large, bony hands, and of great physical power. Many anecdotes of his strength are given, which show that it was equal to that of two or three ordinary men. He lifted with ease five or six hundred pounds. His legs and arms were disproportion-ately long, as compared with his body; and when he walked, he swung his arms to and fro more than most men. When seated, he did not seem much taller than ordinary men. In his movements there was no grace, but an impression of awkward strength and vigor.

He was naturally diffident, and even to the day of his death, when in crowds, and not speaking or acting, and conscious of being observed, he seemed to shrink with bashfulness. When he became interested, or spoke, or

---

* The substance of what follows is from chapter 29th of " The History of Abraham Lincoln, and The Overthrow of Slavery," by Isaac N. Arnold.

listened, this appearance left him, and he indicated no self-consciousness. His forehead was high and broad, his hair very dark, nearly black, and rather stiff and coarse, his eyebrows were heavy, his eyes dark-gray, very expressive and varied; now sparkling with humor and fun, and then deeply sad and melancholy; flashing with indignation at injustice or wrong, and then kind, genial, droll, dreamy; according to his mood.

His nose was large, and clearly defined and well shaped; cheek-bones high and projecting. His mouth coarse, but firm. He was easily caricatured—but difficult to represent as he was, in marble or on canvass. The best bust of him is that of Volk, which was modeled from a cast taken from life in May, 1860, while he was attending court at Chicago.

Among the best portraits, in the judgment of his family and intimate friends, are those of Carpenter, in the picture of the Reading of the Proclamation of Emancipation before the Cabinet, and that of Marshall.

He would be instantly recognized as belonging to that type of tall, thin, large-boned men, produced in the northern portion of the Valley of the Mississippi, and exhibiting its peculiar characteristics in a most marked degree in Illinois, Kentucky and Tennessee. In any crowd in the United States, he would have been readily pointed out as a Western man. His stature, figure, manner, voice, and accent, indicated that he was of the Northwest. His manners were cordial, familiar, genial; always perfectly self-possessed, he made every one feel at home, and no one approached him without being impressed with his kindly, frank nature, his clear, good sense, and his transparent truthfulness and integrity. There is more or less of expression and character in handwriting. Lincoln's was plain, simple, clear, and legible, as that of Washington; but unlike that of Washington, it was without ornament.

4

In endeavoring to state those qualities which gave him success and greatness, among the most important, it seems to me, were a supreme love of truth, and a wonderful capacity to ascertain it. Mentally, he had a perfect eye for truth. His mental vision was clear and accurate: he saw things as they were. I mean that every thing presented to his mind for investigation, he saw divested of every extraneous circumstance, every coloring, association, or accident which could mislead. This gave him at the bar a sagacity which seemed almost instinctive, in sifting the true from the false, and in ascertaining facts; and so it was in all things through life. He ever sought the real, the true, and the right. He was exact, carefully accurate in all his statements. He analyzed well; he saw and presented what lawyers call the very *gist* of every question, divested of all unimportant or accidental relations, so that his statement was a demonstration. At the bar, his exposition of his case, or a question of law, was so clear, that, on hearing it, most persons were surprised that there should be any controversy about it. His reasoning powers were keen and logical, and moved forward to a demonstration with the precision of mathematics. What has been said implies that he possessed not only a sound judgment, which brought him to correct conclusions, but that he was able so to present questions as to bring others to the same result.

His memory was capacious, ready, and tenacious. His reading was limited in extent, but his memory was so ready, and so retentive, that in history, poetry, and general literature, no one ever remarked any deficiency. As an illustration of the power of his memory, I recollect to have once called at the White House, late in his Presidency, and introducing to him a Swede and a Norwegian; he immediately repeated a poem of eight or ten verses, describing Scandinavian scenery and old Norse legends. In reply to the expression of their delight, he said that he had read and admired the poem several years before, and it had entirely gone from him, but seeing them recalled it.

The two books which he read most were the Bible and Shakespeare. With these he was very familiar, reading and studying them habitually and constantly. He had great fondness for poetry, and eloquence, and his taste and judgment in each was exquisite. Shakespeare was his favorite poet; Burns stood next. I know of a speech of his at a Burns festival, in which he spoke at length of Burns's poems; illustrating what he said by many quotations, showing perfect familiarity with and full appreciation of the peasant poet of Scotland. He was extremely fond of ballads, and of simple, sad, and plaintive music.

He was a most admirable reader. He read and repeated passages from the Bible and Shakespeare with great simplicity but remarkable expression and effect. Often when going to and from the army, on steamers and in his carriage, he took a copy of Shakespeare with him, and not unfrequently read, aloud to his associates. After conversing upon public affairs, he would take up his Shakespeare, and addressing his companions, remark, " What do you say now to a scene from Macbeth, or Hamlet, or Julius Cæsar," and then he would read aloud, scene after scene, never seeming to tire of the enjoyment.

On the last Sunday of his life, as he was coming up the Potomac, from his visit to City Point and Richmond, he read aloud many extracts from Shakespeare. Among others, he read, with an accent and feeling which no one who heard him will ever forget, extracts from Macbeth, and among others the following:—

" Duncan is in his grave;
After life's fitful fever, he sleeps well.
Treason has done his worst; nor steel, nor poison,
Malice domestic, foreign levy, nothing
Can touch him farther."

After " treason " had " *done his worst*," the friends who
heard him on that occasion remembered that he read that
passage very slowly over twice, and with an absorbed and
peculiar manner.   Did he feel a mysterious presentiment of
his approaching fate ?

His conversation was original, suggestive, instructive, and
playful; and, by its genial humor,·fascinating and attractive
beyond comparison.   Mirthfulness and sadness were strongly
combined in him.   His mirth was exuberant, it sparkled in
jest, story, and anecdote; and the next moment those peculiarly sad, pathetic, melancholy eyes, showed a man " familiar
with sorrow, and acquainted with grief."   I have listened for
hours at his table, and elsewhere, when he has been surrounded by statesmen, military leaders, and other distinguished men
of the nation, and I but repeat the universally concurring
verdict of all, in stating that as a conversationalist he had no
equal.   One might meet in company with him the most distinguished men, of various pursuits and professions, but after
listening for two or three hours, on separating, it was what
Lincoln had said that would be remembered.   His were the
ideas and illustrations that would not be forgotten.   Men
often called upon him for the pleasure of listening to him.   I
have heard the reply to an invitation to attend the theater,
" No, I am going up to the White House. I would rather
hear Lincoln talk for half an hour, than attend the best
theater in the world."

As a public speaker, without any attempt at oratorical
display, I think he was the most effective of any man of his

day. When he spoke, everybody listened. It was always obvious, before he completed two sentences, that he had something to say, and it was sure to be something original, something different from any thing heard from others, or which had been read in books. He impressed the hearer at once, as an earnest, sincere man, who believed what he said. To-day, there are more of the sayings of Lincoln repeated by the people, more quotations, sentences, and extracts from his writings and speeches, familiar as "household words," than from those of any other American.

I know no book, except the Bible and Shakespeare, from which so many familiar phrases and expressions have been taken as from his writings and speeches. Somebody has said, "I care not who makes the laws, if I may write the ballads of a nation." The words of Lincoln have done more in the last six years to mold and fashion the American character than those of any other man, and their influence has been all for truth, right, justice, and liberty. Great as has been Lincoln's services to the people, as their President, his influence, derived from his words and his example, in molding the future national character, in favor of justice, right, liberty, truth, and real, sincere, unostentatious reverence for God, is scarcely less important. The Republic of the future, the matured national character, will be more influenced by him than by any other man. This is evidence of his greatness, intellectual, and still more, moral. In this power of impressing himself upon the people, he contrasts with many other distinguished men in our history. Few quotations from Jefferson, or Adams, or Webster, live in the every-day language of the people. Little of Clay survives; not much of Calhoun, and who can quote, off-hand, half a dozen sentences from Douglas? But you hear Lincoln's words, not only in every cabin and caucus, and in every stump speech, but at every school-house, high-school, and college declamation, and by every farmer and artisan, as he tells you story after story of Lincoln's, and all to the point, hitting the nail on the head every time, and driving home the argument.   Mr. Lincoln was not a scholar, but where is there a speech more exhaustive in argument than his Cooper Institute address? Where any thing more full of pathos than his farewell to his neighbors at Springfield, when he bade them good-bye, on starting for the capital?   Where any thing more eloquent than his appeal for peace and union, in his first Inaugural, or than his defense of the Declaration of Independence in the Douglas debates? Where the equal of his speech at Gettysburg?   Where a more conclusive argument than in his letter to the Albany Meeting on Arrests?   What is better than his letter to the Illinois State Convention ; and that to Hodges of Kentucky, in explanation of his anti-slavery policy?   Where is there any thing equal in simple grandeur of thought and sentiment, to his last Inaugural?   From all of these, and many others, from his every-day talks, are extracts on the tongues of the people, as familiar, and nearly as much reverenced, as texts from the Bible ; and these are shaping the national character. " Though dead, he yet speaketh."

As a public speaker, if excellence is measured by results, he had no superior.   His manner was generally earnest, often playful ; sometimes, but this was rare, he was vehement and impassioned.   There have been a few instances, at the bar and on the stump, when, wrought up to indignation by some great personal wrong, or by an aggravated case of fraud or injustice, or when speaking of the fearful wrongs and injustice of slavery, he broke forth in a strain of impassioned vehemence which carried every thing before him.

Generally, he addressed the reason and judgment, and the effect was lasting. He spoke extemporaneously, but not without more or less preparation. He had the power of repeating, without reading it, a discourse or speech which he had prepared or written out. His great speech, in opening the Douglas canvass, in June, 1858, was carefully written out, but so naturally spoken that few suspected that it was not extemporaneous. In his style, manner of presenting facts, and way of putting things to the people, he was more like Franklin than any other American. His illustrations, by anecdote and story, were not unlike the author of *Poor Richard.*

A great cause of his intellectual power was the thorough exhaustive investigation he gave to every subject. Take, for illustration, his Cooper Institute speech. Hundreds of able and intelligent men have spoken on the same subject treated by him in that speech, yet what they said will all be forgotten, and his will survive; because his address is absolutely perfect for the purpose for which it was designed. Nothing can be added to it.

Mr. Lincoln, however, required time thoroughly to investigate before he came to his conclusions, and the movements of his mind were not rapid; but when he reached his conclusions he believed in them, and adhered to them with great firmness and tenacity. When called upon to decide quickly upon a new subject or a new point, he often erred, and was ever ready to change when satisfied he was wrong.

It was the union, in Mr. Lincoln, of the capacity clearly to see the truth, and an innate love of truth, and justice, and right in his heart, that constituted his character and made him so great. He never demoralized his intellectual or moral powers, either by doing wrong that good might come, or by advocating error because it was popular. Although, as a statesman, eminently practical, and looking to the possible good of to-day, he ever kept in mind the absolute truth and absolute right, toward which he always aimed.

Mr. Lincoln was an unselfish man; he never sought his own advancement at the expense of others. He was a just man; he never tried to pull others down that he might rise. He disarmed rivalry and envy by his rare generosity. He possessed the rare wisdom of magnanimity. He was eminently a tender-hearted, kind, and humane man. These traits were illustrated all through his life. He loved to pardon: he was averse to punish. It was difficult for him to deny the request of a child, a woman, or of any who were weak and suffering. Pages of incidents might be quoted, showing his ever-thoughtful kindness, gratitude to, and appreciation of the soldiers. The following note (written to a lady known to him only by her sacrifices for her country) is selected from many on this subject:—

"EXECUTIVE MANSION, WASHINGTON,
"November, 1864.

"DEAR MADAM:—

"I have been shown, in the files of the War Department, a statement of the Adjutant-General of Massachusetts, that you are the mother of five sons who have died gloriously on the field of battle. I feel how weak and fruitless must be any words of mine which should attempt to beguile you from the grief of a loss so overwhelming. But I can not refrain from tendering to you the consolation that may be found in the thanks of the Republic they died to save. I pray that our Heavenly Father may assuage the anguish of your bereavement, and leave you only the cherished memory of the loved and lost, and the solemn pride that must be yours to have laid so costly a sacrifice upon the altar of freedom.

"Yours very respectfully,
"ABRAHAM LINCOLN.

"To Mrs. BIXBY, Boston, Massachusetts."

One summer's day, in walking along the shaded path which leads from the White House to the War Department,

I saw the tall form of the President seated on the grass under a tree, with a wounded soldier sitting by his side. He had a bundle of papers in his hand. The soldier had met him in the path, and, recognizing him, had asked his aid. Mr. Lincoln sat down upon the grass, investigated the case, and sent the soldier away rejoicing. In the midst of the rejoicings over the triumphs at Chattanooga and Lookout Mountain, he forgets not to telegraph to Grant, "Remember Burnside" at Knoxville.

His charity, in the best sense of that word, was pervading. When others railed, he railed not again. No bitter words, no denunciation can be found in his writings or speeches. Literally, in his heart there was "malice toward none, and charity for all."

Mr. Lincoln was by nature a gentleman. No man can point, in all his lifetime, to any thing mean, small, tricky, dishonest, or false; on the contrary, he was ever open, manly, brave, just, sincere, and true. That characteristic, attributed to him by some, of coarse story-telling, did not exist. I assert that my intercourse with him was constant for many years before he went to Washington, and I saw him daily, during the greater part of his Presidency; and although his stories and anecdotes were racy, witty, and pointed beyond all comparison, yet I never heard one of a character to need palliation or excuse. If a story had wit and was apt, he did not reject it, because to a vulgar or impure mind it suggested coarse ideas; but he himself was unconscious of any thing but its wit and aptness.

It may interest the people who did not visit Washington during his Presidency, to know something of his habits, and the room he occupied and transacted business in, during his administration. His reception-room was on the second floor, on the south side of the White House, and the second apart-

ment from the southeast corner. The corner room was occupied by Mr. Nicolay, his private secretary; next to this was
the President's reception-room. It was, perhaps, thirty by
twenty feet. In the middle of the west side, was a large
marble fireplace, with old-fashioned brass andirons, and a
large, high, brass fender. The windows looked to the south,
upon the lawn and shrubbery on the south front of the White
House, taking in the unfinished Washington Monument,
Alexandria, the Potomac, and down that beautiful river
toward Mount Vernon. Across the Potomac was Arlington
Heights. The view from these windows was altogether very
beautiful.

The furniture of this room consisted of a long oak table,
covered with cloth, and oak chairs. This table stood in the
center of the room, and was the one around which the Cabinet
sat, at Cabinet meetings, and is faithfully painted in Carpenter's picture of the Emancipation Proclamation. At the end
of the table, near the window, was a large writing-table and
desk, with pigeon-holes for papers, such as are common in
lawyers' offices. In front of this, in a large arm-chair, Mr.
Lincoln usually sat. Behind his chair, and against the west
wall of the room, was another writing-desk high enough to
write upon when standing, and upon the top of this were a
few books, among which were the Statutes of the United
States, a Bible, and a copy of Shakespeare. There was a
bureau, with wooden doors, with pigeon-holes for papers,
standing between the windows. Here the President kept
such papers as he wished readily to refer to. There were
two plain sofas in the room; generally two or three map-
frames, from which hung military maps, on which the movements of the armies were continually traced and followed.
The only picture in the room was an old engraving of Jack-

son, which hung over the fireplace; late in his administration was added a fine photograph of John Bright. Two doors opened into this room—one from the Secretary's, the other from the great hall, where the crowd usually waited. A bell-cord hung within reach of his hand, while he sat at his desk. There was an ante-room adjoining this, plainly furnished; but the crowd usually pressed to the hall, from which an entrance might be directly had to the President's room. A messenger stood at the door, and took in the cards and names of visitors.

Here, in this room, more plainly furnished than many law and business offices—plainer than the offices of the heads of bureaus in the Executive Departments—Mr. Lincoln spent the days of his Presidency. Here he received everybody, from the Lieutenant-General and Chief-Justice, down to the private soldier and humblest citizen. Custom had established certain rules of precedence, fixing the order in which officials should be received. The members of the Cabinet and the high officers of the army were, of course, received always promptly. Senators and members of Congress, who are usually charged with the presentation of petitions and recommendations for appointments, and who are expected to right every wrong and correct every evil each one of their respective constituents may be suffering, or imagine himself to be suffering, have an immense amount of business with the Executive. I have often seen as many as ten or fifteen Senators and twenty or thirty Members of the House in the hall, waiting their turn to see the President. They would go to the ante-room, or up to the hall in front of the reception-room, and await their turns. The order of precedence was, first the Vice-President, if present, then the Speaker of the House, and then Senators and Members of the House in the order of their arrival, and the presentation of their cards. Fre-

quently Senators and Members would go to the White House
as early as eight or nine in the morning, to secure precedence
and an early interview. While they waited, the loud ringing laugh of Mr. Lincoln, in which he was sure to be joined
by all *inside*, but which was rather provoking to those *out-
side*, was often heard by the waiting and impatient crowd.
Here, from early morning to late at night, he sat, listened,
and decided—patient, just, considerate, hopeful. All the
people came to him as to a father. He was more accessible
than any of the leading members of his Cabinet—much more
so than Mr. Seward, shut up in the State Department, writing
his voluminous dispatches; far more so than Mr. Stanton, in-
defatigable, stern, abrupt, but ever honest and faithful. Mr.
Lincoln saw everybody — governors, senators, congressmen,
officers, ministers, bankers, merchants, farmers—all classes of
people; all approached him with confidence, from the highest
to the lowest; but this incessant labor and fearful responsibility told upon his vigorous frame. He left Illinois for the
capital, with a frame of iron and nerves of steel. His old
friends, who knew him in Illinois as a man who knew not
what illness was, who knew him ever genial and sparkling
with fun, as the months and years of the war passed slowly
on, saw the wrinkles on his forehead deepened into furrows;
and the laugh of old days became sometimes almost hollow;
it did not now always seem to come from the heart, as in
former years. Anxiety, responsibility, care, thought, wore
upon even his giant frame, and his nerves of steel became at
times irritable. For more than four years he had no respite,
no holidays. When others fled away from the dust and heat
of the capital, he must stay; he would not leave the helm
until the danger was past and the ship was in port.

Mrs. Lincoln watched his care-worn face with the anxiety

of an affectionate wife, and sometimes took him. from his labors almost in spite of himself. She urged him to ride, and to go to the theater and places of amusement, to divert his mind from his engrossing cares.

Let us for a moment try to appreciate the greatness of his work and his services. He was the Commander-in-Chief, during the war, of the largest army and navy in the world; and this army and navy was created during his administration, and its officers were sought out and appointed by him. The operations of the Treasury were vast beyond all previous conceptions of the ability of the country to sustain; and yet, when he entered upon the Presidency, he found an empty treasury, the public credit shaken, no army, no navy, the officers all strangers, many deserting, more in sympathy with the rebels, Congress divided, and public sentiment unformed. The party which elected him were in a minority. The old Democratic party, which had ruled the country for half a century, hostile to him, and, by long political association, in sympathy with the insurgent States. His own party, new, made up of discordant elements, and not yet consolidated, unaccustomed to rule, and neither his party nor himself possessing any *prestige*. He entered the White House, the object of personal prejudice to a majority of the people, and of contempt to a powerful minority. And yet, I am satisfied, from the statement of the conversation of Mr. Lincoln with Mr. Bateman, quoted hereafter, and from various other reasons, that he himself more fully appreciated the terrible conflict before him than any man in the nation, and that even then he hoped and expected to be the *Liberator* of the slaves. He did not yet clearly perceive the manner in which it was to be done, but he believed it would be done, and that God would guide him.

In four years, this man crushed the most stupendous rebellion, supported by armies more vast, and resources greater
than were ever before combined to overthrow any government.   He held together and consolidated, against warring
factions, his own great party, and strengthened it by securing
the confidence and bringing to his aid a large proportion of
all other parties.   He was re-elected almost by acclamation,
and he led the people, step by step, up to emancipation, and
saw his work crowned by the Constitutional Amendment,
eradicating Slavery from the Republic for ever.   Did this
man lack firmness?   Study the boldness of the Emancipation!   See with what fidelity he stood by his Proclamation!   In his message of 1863, he said : " I will *never* retract
the proclamation, nor return to slavery any person made free
by it."   In 1864, he said : " If it should ever be made a duty
of the Executive to return to slavery any person made free
by the Proclamation or the acts of Congress, some other person, not I, must execute the law."

When hints of peace were suggested as obtainable by
giving over the negro race again to bondage, he repelled it
with indignation.   When the rebel Vice-President, Stephens,
at Fortress Monroe, tempted him to give up the freedmen,
and seek the glory of a foreign war, in which the Union and
Confederate soldiers might join, neither party sacrificing its
honor, he was inflexible ; he would die sooner than break
the nation's plighted faith.

Mr. Lincoln did not enter with reluctance upon the plan
of emancipation ; and in this statement I am corroborated by
Lovejoy and Sumner, and many others.   If he did not act
more promptly, it was because he knew he must not go faster
than the people.   Men have questioned the firmness, boldness, and will of Mr. Lincoln.   He had no vanity in the ex-

hibition of power, but he quietly acted, when he felt it his duty so to do, with a boldness and firmness never surpassed.

What bolder act than the surrender of Mason and Slidell, against the resolution of Congress and the almost universal popular clamor, without consulting the Senate or taking advice from his Cabinet?* The removals of McClellan and Butler, the modification of the orders of Fremont and Hunter, were acts of a bold, decided character. He acted for himself, taking personally the responsibility of deciding the great questions of his administration.

He was the most democratic of all the presidents. Personally, he was homely, plain, without pretension, and without ostentation. He believed in the people, and had faith in their good impulses. He ever addressed himself to their reason, and not to their prejudices. His language was simple, sometimes quaint, never sacrificing expression to elegance. When he spoke to the people, it was as though he said to them, "Come, let us reason together." There can not be found in all his speeches or writings a single vulgar expression, nor an appeal to any low sentiment or prejudice. He had nothing of the demagogue. He never himself alluded to his humble origin, except to express regret for the deficiencies of his education. He always treated the people in such a way, that they knew that he respected them, believed them honest, capable of judging correctly, and disposed to do right.

I know not how, in a few words, I can better indicate his political and moral character, than by the following incident: A member of Congress, knowing the purity of his life, his reverence for God, and his respect for religion, one day expressed surprise, that he had not joined a church. After mentioning some difficulties he felt in regard to some articles of faith, Mr. Lincoln said, " *Whenever any church* will inscribe over its altar, as its sole qualification for membership, Christ's condensed statement of both Law and Gospel, '*Thou shalt love the Lord, thy God with all thy heart, and with all thy soul, and with all thy mind, and thy neighbor as thyself*,' that church will I join with all my heart."

Love to God, as the great Father, love to man as his brother, constituted the basis of his political and moral creed.

One day, when one of his friends was denouncing his political enemies, "Hold on," said Mr. Lincoln, "Remember what St. Paul says, 'and now abideth faith, hope, charity, these three; *but the greatest of these is charity.*'"

From the day of his leaving Springfield to assume the duties of the Presidency, when he so impressively asked his friends and neighbors to invoke upon him the guidance and wisdom of God, to the evening of his death, he seemed ever to live and act in the consciousness of his responsibility to Him, and with the trusting faith of a child he leaned confidingly upon His Almighty Arm. He was visited during his administration by many Christian delegations, representing the various religious denominations of the Republic, and it is known that he was relieved and comforted in his great work by the consciousness that the Christian world were praying for his success. Some one said to him, one day, "No man was ever so remembered in the prayers of the people, especially of those who pray not to be heard of men, as you are." He replied, "I have been a good deal helped by just that thought."

The support which Mr. Lincoln received during his administration from the religious organizations, and the sympathy and confidence between the great body of Christians and the President, was indeed a source of immense strength and power to him.

I know of nothing revealing more of the true character of

Mr. Lincoln, his conscientiousness, his views of the slavery question, his sagacity and his full appreciation of the awful trial through which the country and he had to pass, than the following incident stated by Mr. Bateman, Superintendent of Public Instruction for Illinois.

On one occasion, in the autumn of 1860, after conversing with Mr. Bateman at some length, on the, to him, strange con-duct of Christian men and ministers of the Gospel supporting slavery, he said:—

"I know there is a God, and that He hates injustice and slavery. I see the storm coming, and I know that His hand is in it. If He has a place and work for me—and I think He has—I believe I am ready. I am nothing, but truth is every thing. I know I am right, because I know that Liberty is right, for Christ teaches it, and Christ is God. I have told them that a house divided against itself can not stand; and Christ and Reason say the same; and they will find it so.

"Douglas don't care whether slavery is voted up or down, but God cares, and humanity cares, and I care; and with God's help I shall not fail. I may not see the end; but it will come, and I shall be vindicated; and these men will find that they have not read their Bibles right."

Much of this was uttered as if he were speaking to him-self, and with a sad, earnest solemnity of manner impossible to be described. After a pause, he resumed: "Doesn't it appear strange that men can ignore the moral aspect of this contest? A revelation could not make it plainer to me that, slavery or the Government must be destroyed. The future would be something awful, as I look at it, but for this rock on which I stand (alluding to the Testament which he still held in his hand). It seems as if God had borne with this thing (slavery) until the very teachers of religion had come to de-

5

fend it from the Bible, and to claim for it a divine character
and sanction; and now the cup of iniquity is full, and the
vials of wrath will be poured out." After this, says Mr. Bateman, the conversation was continued for a long time. Every
thing he said was of a peculiarly deep, tender, and religious
tone, and all was tinged with a touching melancholy. He
repeatedly referred to his conviction that the day of wrath
was at hand, and that he was to be an actor in the terrible
struggle which would issue in the overthrow of slavery,
though he might not live to see the end.*

Perhaps in all history there is no example of such great
and long continued injustice as that of the British press
during the war toward Mr. Lincoln. His death shamed them
into decency. While he lived they sneered at his manners.
Let them turn to their own Cromwell. They said his person was
ugly. Has the world recognized the ability of Mirabeau, or
that of Henry Brougham, notwithstanding their ugliness?
They made scurrile jests about his figure, as though a statesman must be necessarily a sculptor's model! They were
facetious about his dress, as though a greater than a Fox or a
Chatham must be a Beau Brummel. They were horrified
by his jokes. If the same had been told by the patrician
Palmerston, instead of the plebeian Lincoln, they would not
have lacked the "Attic salt," but would have rivaled Dean
Swift or Sidney Smith.

It has been truly said there is one parallel only, to English
journalism's treatment of Lincoln, and that is to be found in
their treatment of Napoleon. "The Corsican Ogre," and the
"American Ape," were phrases coined in the same mint. But
the great Corsican was England's bitter foe; Lincoln was

---

* The foregoing statement has been verified by Mr. Bateman as substantially
correct.

never provoked either by his own or his country's wrongs, to hostility against Great Britain. Yet at the great Martyr's grave, even this injustice changed to respect and reverence; even "Punch" repented and said—

> "Yes he had lived to shame me from my sneer,
>   To lame my pencil, and confute my pen;
>   To make me own this hind, of princes *peer*,
>   This rail-splitter a true-born *King* of men."

The place Mr. Lincoln will occupy in history, will be higher than any which he held while living. His Emancipation Proclamation is the most important historical event of the nineteenth century. Its influence will not be limited by time, nor bounded by locality. It will ever be treated by the historian as one of the great landmarks of human progress.

He has been compared and contrasted with three great personages in history, who were assassinated,—with Cæsar, with William of Orange, and with Henry IV. of France. He was a nobler type of man than either, as he was the product of a higher and more Christian civilization.

The two great men by whose words and example our great continental Republic is to be fashioned and shaped are Washington and Lincoln. Representative men of the East, and of the West, of the Revolutionary era, and the era of Liberty for all. One sleeps upon the banks of the Potomac, and the other on the great prairies of the Valley of the Mississippi. Lincoln was as pure as Washington, as modest, as just, as patriotic; less passionate by nature, more of a democrat in his feelings and manners, with more faith in the people, and more hopeful of their future. Statesmen and patriots will study their record and learn the wisdom of goodness.

ENGRAVED PORTRAIT OF PRESIDENT LINCOLN.

THE Portrait of Mr. LINCOLN, accompanying this book, has been engraved, for the Publisher, expressly for it. No labor or expense has been spared to produce a First-Class Engraving. It was executed by H. B. HALL, JR., ESQ., who unquestionably stands in the front rank of American Engravers. The great Painting of

"The Last Hours of Lincoln,"

is now being engraved by Mr. HALL, in the same style.

This PORTRAIT of President LINCOLN is pronounced by all to be the most life-like—the best ever engraved of him. It may not be improper to state that I have a letter from his family to that effect, which I refrain to place in print. I will, however, publish a few from persons intimately acquainted with him, selecting from the large number that I have received.

Engraved Portrait of President Lincoln.

"WASHINGTON, D. C., *June 22, 1868.*

"DEAR SIR:—

"I have examined with interest the steel engraving of President LINCOLN published by you. I knew him intimately more than thirty years, being at times a member of his family.

"I regard this portrait the happiest likeness—and it conveys to me the most pleasing recollection of ABRAHAM LINCOLN of any that I have seen.

"Very truly yours,
"J. B. S. TODD.

"COL. JOHN B. BACHELDER."

"TREASURY DEPARTMENT, WASHINGTON, D. C., *July 30, 1868.*

"DEAR SIR:—

"I have carefully examined the portrait of the late President, Mr. LINCOLN, engraved by Mr. H. B. HALL, Jr., and published by yourself. The engraving is exceedingly fine, and the *likeness* is superior to any that I have seen. As a work of Art, it is in the highest degree creditable to Mr. HALL.

"Very respectfully,
"HUGH McCULLOCH,
"*Secretary of the Treasury.*

"COL. JOHN B. BACHELDER."

"WAR DEPARTMENT, *July 30, 1868.*

" * * * It is one of the most truthful likenesses of the late President that I have seen. * * *

"Yours very truly,
"J. M. SCHOFIELD,
"*Secretary of War.*

"COL. JOHN B. BACHELDER."

"NAVY DEPARTMENT, *July 30, 1868.*

" * * * I think it a correct and satisfactory likeness in all respects.

"GIDEON WELLES,
"*Secretary of Navy.*

"J. B. BACHELDER, ESQ."

"HEAD-QUARTERS, CORPS OF ENGINEERS,
"WASHINGTON, D. C., *July 30, 1868.*

" * * * It is a beautiful piece of Art, indeed it is I think quite remarkable, presenting, as it does that characteristic expression of the eye as well as of the features and lines of the face. * * *

"I am very truly yours,
"A. A. HUMPHREYS,
"*Major-General.*"

A quarto edition of this Engraving has been published, suitable to frame, which will be sent free by mail to any part of the country on the reception of the price.

STYLE AND PRICES.

PRINT, $1.00; PLAIN PROOF, $2.00; INDIA PROOF, $3.00; ARTIST'S PROOF (selected and signed by the engraver, and tastefully framed in a *passe-partout*), $5.00. (Express delivery extra.)

Orders Addressed to

JOHN B. BACHELDER, Publisher,

59 BEEKMAN STREET, NEW YORK.

PROSPECTUS OF WORKS

PUBLISHED BY

JOHN B. BACHELDER,

59 BEEKMAN STREET,

NEW YORK.

COL. MORROW, with the COLORS of the 24th MICH. VOLS.

GETTYSBURG.

WHEN a person is desirous of procuring a published work upon any subject, it is natural for him to inquire for the sources of information from which the author has compiled that work. I have, therefore, without wishing to be considered egotistical, concluded to issue this prospectus to such as have an interest in the Battle of Gettysburg, that they may know what I have already done, and what I yet propose to do. to eliminate the history of that battle.

ISOMETRICAL DRAWING OF THE GETTYSBURG BATTLE-FIELD.

In compiling the Isometrical Drawing of the Gettysburg Battle-field, it was first necessary to establish its extent and boundaries. When I arrived at Gettysburg the *debris* of that great battle lay scattered for miles around. Fresh mounds of earth marked the resting-place of the fallen thousands, and many of the dead lay yet unburied. It therefore required no guide to point out the locality where the battle had been fought.

As the term *field*, when applied to a battle, is generally used figuratively, and, by the general reader, might be misunderstood, it is well to consider at the start, that the battle-*field* of Gettysburg not only embraces within its boundaries many *fields*, but forests as well, and even the town of Gettysburg itself is included in that battle-field. The formation of the ground and the positions of the troops, favored the plan of sketching the field while facing the west. Consequently the top of my DRAWING of it is west; the right hand, north; the left, south, &c. There was no point from which the whole field could be sketched, nor would such a position have favored this branch of Art. On the contrary, it was necessary to sketch from *every* part of the field, combining the whole into one grand view.

DEATH OF GEN. ZOOK.

Having located its boundaries, I commenced at the southeast corner, and gradually moving toward the *north*, I looked toward the *west*, and sketched it carefully, as far as the vision extended, including fields, forests, houses, barns, hills, and valleys; and every object, however minute, which would influence the result of a battle. Thus I continued to the northeast boundary, a distance of five and a half miles. The next day I resumed my work at the south (having advanced to the point where my vision had been obstructed the preceding day), and sketched another breadth to the north, as before; and so continued, day by day, until I had carried my Drawing forward four and a half miles, which included within its limits the town of Gettysburg. When the Battle-field had been *Isometrically* drawn, I sketched in the *distance* and added a sky.

This Drawing was the result of eighty-four days spent on that field immediately after the battle, during which time I sketched accurately the twenty-five
square miles which it represents.

I spent two months in hospital writing down the statements of Confederate prisoners, and as they became convalescent, I went over the field with many
of their officers, who located their positions and explained the movements of their
commands during the battle.

I then visited the ARMY OF THE POTOMAC, consulted with its Commander-in-
Chief, Corps, Division, and Brigade commanders, and visited every Regiment and
Battery, engaged, to whose officers the sketch of the field was submitted, and they,
after careful consultation, located upon it the positions of their respective commands.

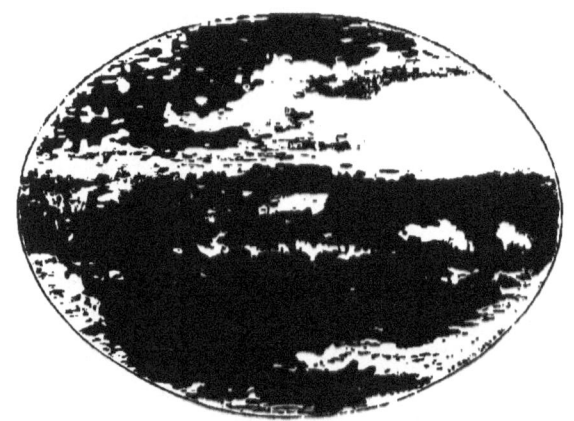

PHILLIPS' 5th MASS. BATTERY

From the information thus obtained, I have traced the movements of *every
Regiment and Battery* from the commencement to the close of the battle, and
have located on the Drawing its most important position for each of the three
days.

Since its publication I issued an invitation to the officers of the Army of the
Potomac to visit Gettysburg with me, and point out their respective positions and
movements, thus giving an opportunity to the *actors* in this great drama to correct
any misapprehension, and establish, while still fresh in memory, the facts and
details of this most important battle of the age. This invitation was responded to
by over one thousand officers engaged in the battle; twenty-eight of whom were
Generals commanding. And it may be interesting to those who possess the Drawing, to know that *but one solitary Regiment* was discovered to be out of position
on it.

Many thousand copies of this work have been sold, yet the demand still continues, and orders are constantly coming in from all parts of the country. Though complete in itself, it is really but the *introduction* to other works yet to be published on this battle, and will be considered almost an indispensable companion to the history of it.

It can be furnished at the following.:

PRICES.

COLORED PROOF. on heavy plate paper, carefully finished in Water-Colors, $15 00

PROOF, printed in tints, on paper as above, with positions of Regiments,

colored, - - - - - - - - - - - - 10 00

TINTED, printed with one tint, on lighter paper, - - - - - 5 00

☞ The above styles have a sky, and are suitable to frame, and are accompanied by a key.

PLAIN, on lighter paper, without sky, - - - - - - - $3 00

CAPTURE OF THE 8th LA. COLORS BY LT. YOUNG, ADG'T 107th OHIO VOLS.

The original plate has not been used except to print copies for *transfers*. The *first* impressions from each transfer are reserved for PROOFS. Therefore the quality of the print can never materially change, as the original plate would furnish a thousand transfers. The *colored* PROOFS are carefully colored by an Artist. The TINTED and PLAIN editions are next printed, and when the plate is worn a new transfer is made.

To any person remitting the money, for either of the above styles, I will forward the print by mail, to any part of the United States, FREE OF CHARGE, carefully packed on a roll; or, I will send it by express, at their expense, with bill for collection. I have sent hundreds by mail, to all parts of the country, and have yet to hear of the first copy being lost or injured, while it is quite a saving of expense. A *Key*, embracing a brief description of the battle, accompanies each print without extra charge. I have hundreds of letters of indorsement from which I select the following:—

TESTIMONIALS.

"HEAD-QUARTERS ARMY OF THE POTOMAC. *Feb.* 11, 1864.

"I have examined Col. Bachelder's ISOMETRICAL DRAWING of the Gettysburg Battle-field, and am perfectly satisfied with the accuracy with which the topography is delineated, and the positions of the troops laid down. Col. B., in my judgment, deserves great credit for the time and labor he has devoted to obtaining the materials for this drawing, which have resulted in making it so accurate. * * * * I can cheerfully recommend it to all those who are desirous of procuring an accurate picture and faithful record of the events of this great battle. * * * *

"I remain most truly yours,

"GEO. G. MEADE,
"*Maj.-Gen. Comd'g. A. P.*"

"HEAD-QUARTERS SECOND ARMY CORPS, *Dec.* 29, 1863.

"The view of the Battle-field of Gettysburg prepared by Col. Bachelder, has been carefully examined by me. I find it as accurate as such a drawing can well be made. And *it is accurate*, as far as my knowledge extends.

"WINF'D S. HANCOCK,
"*Major-General Comd'g 2d Corps.*"

"Col. Bachelder's Isometrical View of the Battle of Gettysburg is an admirable production, and a truthful rendering of the various positions assumed by the troops of my command.

"A. DOUBLEDAY,
Maj.-Gen. Vols., Comd'g 1st Corps."

"BOSTON, *Sept.* 23, 1864.

"COL. BACHELDER:—I have examined your beautiful drawing of the Battle-field of Gettysburg and vicinity. The certificates of Gen. Meade and the Corps Commanders, which appear on its face, establish its accuracy on the highest authority. Your personal explorations, and your inquiries of all the commissioned officers in command of the Union Army, and of the Confederate officers made prisoners, have furnished you means of information not possessed, I imagine, by any other person. Such opportunities of observation as I had during three days passed at Gettysburg satisfy me of the fidelity of your delineation of the position of every regiment of the two armies on each of the three eventful days. * * * * I may add, that the engraving is beautifully executed and colored. Wishing you ample remuneration,

"I remain sincerely yours,

"EDWARD EVERETT."

"HEAD-QUARTERS FIFTH ARMY CORPS, *Sept.* 28, 1864.

"MR. JNO. B. BACHELDER:—

"DEAR SIR:—I am exceedingly gratified with receiving a finished copy of your print of the Battle-field of Gettysburg. I am familiar with your long and untiring labors in all the fields where truth could be reached, and know that your efforts were crowned with a success that leaves nothing more to be desired. You are authorized to add my name to those who bear testimony to its accuracy.

"Very respectfully your obedient servant,

"G. K. WARREN,
"*Maj.-Gen. Vols., Comd'g 5th Corps.*
"*Ch. Eng. at Gettysburg.*"

"ORANGE, *Oct.* 1, 1864.

"JNO. B. BACHELDER, Esq.:—

"MY DEAR SIR:—I have carefully examined your Isometrical Drawing of the Battle-field of Gettysburg, with great interest and much profit. Never having been on that field, of course I can not express an opinion as to its accuracy—so abundantly indorsed for, however, by most competent judges; but I can say that it has given me a much clearer idea of the battle than I had before, and I earnestly hope that you will find it convenient to illustrate others of our great battles in the same manner.

"I am very truly yours,

"GEO. B. McCLELLAN."

"MR. JNO. B. BACHELDER:—

"MY DEAR SIR:—I was much gratified on receiving a copy of your beautiful drawing of the 'Gettysburg Battle-field.' I have never seen a painting or topographical map that could give so vivid a representation of a great battle. I regard it as an honor that you have associated my name with those of other corps commanders in your historical picture. Be pleased to accept my kind regards.

"Respectfully yours,

"O. O. HOWARD, *Major-General.*"

"COL. JNO. B. BACHELDER:—

"DEAR SIR:—I have examined with care your Isometrical Drawing of the Gettysburg Battle-field, and can cheerfully bear testimony to the accuracy of the position of the troops on the right of our line.

"Yours very truly,

"H. W. SLOCUM,

"*Maj.-Gen. Vols., Com'd'g Right Wing at Gettysburg.*"

WOFFORD'S FLANK ATTACK ON SWEITZER'S BRIGADE, DEATH OF COL. JEFFERS
4th MICH. VOLS.

HISTORY OF THE BATTLE.

During my consultations with officers at the front, as well as on the Battle-field, I noted down with great care their conversations, and have books full of material thus rescued from oblivion.

Since the publication of the Drawing, and even before, I have been steadily engaged in compiling the History of the Battle of Gettysburg. I have traveled many thousand miles to add to my knowledge. I have received a great number of letters relating to it, and the Government have very considerately placed at my disposal the entire Reports of both the Union and Confederate officers; and have also given me access to the archives at Washington. They have recently ordered a re-survey of the field, which is now being done by Government Engineers in the most complete and scientific manner. A fine Topographical map is to be com-

STANNARD'S BRIGADE OPENING ON PICKETTS' DIVISION.

piled and engraved, copies of which I have arranged to have to illustrate my History of the Battle. This book, in addition to the maps, which will cost several thousand dollars, will also be illustrated with Steel Plates and Wood-Cuts in a manner second to no book heretofore published in this country. Over $7,500 worth of illustrations are already engraved to embellish it, including fine Steel Portraits, executed by the best engravers in America, in line and stipple, of Generals Reynolds, Doubleday, Newton, Meredith, Stannard, Hancock, Gibbon, Zook, Hays, Webb, Hall, Sickles, Birney, Humphreys, Berdan, Sykes, Barnes, Tilton, Wright, Bartlett, Wheaton, Howard, Ames, Slocum, Williams, Geary, Kane, Pleasanton, Butterfield, Warren, Hunt, Ingalls, Randolph, Martin, and Me-

Gilvrey. Several others are in hand, and undoubtedly more will be added to the list. In addition to these the Portraits of leading Confederate Generals will be engraved. Many of the prominent scenes of the battle have already been beautifully designed and engraved on wood, samples of which embellish this circular, others are to be added, and to those interested I shall be pleased to furnish full information regarding either portraits or wood-cuts.

I shall publish a POPULAR EDITION of the history, with portraits printed from transfers, and bound in cloth. Price......... .... $7 50

The next will be the LIBRARY EDITION, royal octavo, printed on good fair paper, good plates, and substantially bound in sheep.................... $12 00

The same size printed on fine paper. Proof Portraits—bound in half morocco, beveled boards.. $17 50

A FINE EDITION on tinted paper. Proof Portraits. Full morocco, gilt, beveled boards, gilt edges................................. .... $25 00

A LARGE PAPER EDITION (limited) will be printed from new type, and the original wood-cuts in the best style of modern hand-press work, on heavy toned paper, with the finest INDIA PROOF PORTRAITS. In Sheets, stitched, uncut, $100 00

Elaborately bound. Full levant morocco, gilt.................... $125 00

I have now devoted five years and a half to collecting material for the history of the Battle of Gettysburg, but until quite recently I have felt unwilling to commence to write, knowing that other matter existed which it was important for me to have, and which, when obtained, might make a material change in the account. This reason no longer exists, though I shall still thankfully receive suggestions from any participant in the battle.

Within another year the Government will have completed the Topographical Map of the field, by which time I hope to be ready to publish my work. As a publisher I would have done so long ago, but as a historian not until I feel that I have written the truth—the whole truth, and nothing but the truth.

PAINTINGS OF THE BATTLE.

I have also in progress, the finest Collection of Oil Paintings executed of any battle in this country. The whole to be known as

"THE GETTYSBURG ART GALLERY."

I have divided the Battle into a series of episodes, beginning with its commencement and continuing to its close, each to embrace such movements and operations as of themselves form a complete unit. Of each, I make an accurate historical design, which design I place in the hands of some eminent battle-scene painter, who will be responsible for the artistic rendering of the subject. Each painting is to be 7×4 ft., and when completed, will be exhibited in the places

REPULSE OF LONGSTREET'S CHARGE.

where the regiments represented in it were raised. The whole, together, will form a most complete and graphic representation of the Battle from its commencement to the close. Each of these paintings will be engraved on steel, and hereafter engravings may be had representing actual scenes, which, having been designed under the personal direction of the participants themselves, will possess the merit of historical truth.

It must not be understood that this whole work is to be put in hand at once. It will be taken up in detail, and continued as rapidly as I have time and means to attend to it. I shall be happy to correspond with those interested in any portion of the Battle. When convenient, it will be better to call a meeting, at Gettysburg, of the officers of the command to be represented, before commencing a painting, that all the details may be properly arranged. I have already made a design, representing the "charge" of the 6th Wisconsin, 95th N. Y., and 14th N. Y. S. M., on the first day, resulting in the capture of the 2d Mississippi Regiment, which is now being painted by Alonzo Chappel, Esq., the eminent historical painter. I have recently met, at Gettysburg, the officers of the 3d Division, 1st Army Corps, and under their direction completed a design of their engagement on the afternoon of the first day, which will also embrace the movements of the 1st Brigade, 1st Division. This picture is now being painted by the distinguished battle-scene painter, James Walker, Esq.

Fine Steel Engravings will be published from these paintings. Size (engraved surface), 12 × 21 in.

PRICES:

Prints, $5.00 ; Plain Proofs, $10.00 ; India Proofs, $15.00 ; Artist's Proofs, $25.00.

DEATH OF MAJOR FERRY, 5th MICH. CAV'Y.

Mr. Walker has just completed for me, his graphic representation of

THE REPULSE OF LONGSTREET'S CHARGE,

on the afternoon of the third day, which will be exhibited in the principal cities of the country. This is also from my historical design, and has been painted under my immediate direction. Mr. Walker spent weeks at Gettysburg, transcribing the portraiture of the field to canvas, which has been done in the most pleasing and lifelike manner. We have received in this matter the kindest support and co-operation of the officers of the army, engaged on that portion of the field.

Many distinguished general officers, on my invitation, visited Gettysburg, and went over the field with us, and pointed out all the details of this great turning point of the Rebellion; each explaining the movements of their several commands. Among those present at different times, were Generals Meade, Hancock, Gibbon, Howard, Doubleday, Stannard, Hunt, Warren, Humphreys, Graham, Burling, De Trobriand, Wistar, and Dana; together with a large number of Field, Line, and Staff-Officers. Most of these gentlemen have since kindly called at Mr. Walker's studio, and aided the work with their advice. Many others, who were unable to meet with us at Gettysburg, have, at considerable trouble, visited the studio in New York; among them, Generals Webb, Hall, Newton, Hazard, Sickles, Ward, Brewster, Berdan, and Gates, and Generals Wilcox and Longstreet, of the Confederate Army; the latter taking great interest in the painting, and leaving me a fine letter indorsing its accuracy. This painting has been designed *strictly* in conformity to the directions of these gentlemen, given on the field for that purpose, and from the Reports of the Confederate Commanders, furnished to me by the Government.

This great representative Battle-scene has not its equal in America, for correctness of design or accuracy of execution. Gibbon's and Hays's Divisions and the Corps Artillery, occupy the immediate foreground. It is on a canvas $7\frac{1}{2} \times 20$ feet, and represents, not only every Regiment engaged at that portion of the field, but where the formation of the ground would admit, the entire left wing is shown.

It presents such an accurate and lifelike portrait of the country, that on it the movements of the first and second day's operations can readily be traced. No important scene has been screened behind large foreground figures, or, for the want of a knowledge of the details, hidden by convenient puffs of smoke; but every feature of this gigantic struggle has, in its proper place, been woven into a symmetrical whole.

A fine steel plate is also to be engraved of this picture, which will be accompanied by a *Key*, by which the position of every Regiment and Battery can be determined.

PRICE OF ENGRAVINGS.

Print, $10.—Plain Proof, $25.—India Proof, $60.—Artist Proof (limited to 200 copies), $100.

The following gentlemen, intimately identified with the Battle of Gettysburg, and exercising the highest commands at the battle, kindly furnished me these letters, as indorsements to an application to examine Confederate Reports of the Battle of Gettysburg, at the War Department.

" GENERAL :—

" * * * * Mr. Bachelder has accumulated a vast amount of official and reliable testimony on our side, and I am of the opinion his work will be as truthful as the data in his possession will admit ; I am greatly interested in his application being granted, and would most earnestly recommend permission being given him to examine the Confederate Reports, in case you do not see any strong reasons preventing it.

" Very truly yours,

"GEO. G. MEADE,

" *Major-General, U. S. A.*

" GENERAL U. S. GRANT,
" *Sec. War, ad interim.*"

☞ PERMISSION GRANTED.

[Extract of a letter from Major-General Humphreys, Chief of the Corps of Engineers.]

" WASHINGTON, D. C., *Nov.* 14, 1867.

" GENERAL :—

" * * * The information which Mr. Bachelder has collected concerning the Battle of Gettysburg, is extraordinary in amount and correctness. So far as I am able to judge, there is no battle of any war respecting which so many truthful accounts, so many exact details, have been collected and compiled. From every source, from the private to the general commanding the army, facts have been collected, and where discrepancies were found, evidence was multiplied, and in this way errors have been dissipated.

Mr. Bachelder has peculiar qualifications for the task he has undertaken, and has devoted four years to it. * * *

"A. A. HUMPHREYS,

"*Major-General.*

" GENERAL U. S. GRANT,
" *Sec. of War, ad interim.*"

DEATH OF PRIVATE RIGGIN, GUIDON BEARER, RICKETTS' (PA) BATTERY

NOTE.—The wood-cuts interspersed through this circular have been engraved to illustrate scenes in the Battle of Gettysburg, and with many others will appear in the History of that Battle.

"THE LAST HOURS OF LINCOLN."

ORIGIN OF THIS HISTORICAL PAINTING.

ABRAHAM LINCOLN, President of the United States, was assassinated by JOHN WILKES BOOTH, on the night of April 14, 1865, at Ford's Theater, Washington, D. C. This night, fraught with woe to the peoples of two continents, sombered by its halo of diabolism, must forever remain the Golgotha of American history.

At the threshold of the temple of peace—the High Priest was stricken down—and the great heart whose every throb was a pulsation of love for his country's enemies, was robed in silence. In company with Mrs. LINCOLN, Miss HARRIS, and Major RATHBONE, Mr. LINCOLN had sought a brief respite from the iron wheel of State toil, and in the search, through the medium of the assassin's bullet, found a respite for all time.

Immediately after the fatal shot was fired, and under direction of Assistant-Surgeons LEALE and TAFT, he was removed to a private house, and placed upon a couch in a small bedroom. ROBERT LINCOLN, General TODD, and Dr. TODD, cousins of Mrs. LINCOLN, and other personal friends, speedily arrived. His family physician, Dr. STONE, and Surgeon-General BARNES, accompanied by Asst.-Surgeon General CRANE, were in early attendance, and later he was visited by Drs. HALL and LIEBERMANN, and other eminent physicians, all of whom agreed that the wound was unto death. The bullet had entered the back of his head, and lodged behind the right eye.

Mr. LINCOLN was visited during the night by Vice-President JOHNSON and the entire cabinet, except Mr. SEWARD, including Secretaries McCULLOCH, STANTON, WELLES, and USHER, Postmaster-General DENNISON, and Attorney-General SPEED, together with Asst.-Secretaries FIELD, ECKERT, and OTTO. There were also present, Speaker COLFAX, Chief-Justice CARTTER, Senator WILSON, Representatives FARNSWORTH, ARNOLD, MARSTON, and ROLLINS, Governor OGLESBY, accompanied by Adjutant-General HAYNIE, Major HAY, Generals AUGER, MEIGS, and HALLECK, Ex-Governor FARWELL, Rev. Dr. GURLEY, and Commissioner FRENCH, Colonels VINCENT PELOUZE and RUTHERFORD, and Major ROCKWELL. Early in the night Mrs. LINCOLN sent for Mrs. Senator DIXON, who was accompanied by her sister and niece, Mrs. KINNEY and daughter. There were also a few others present during the night, but never more than half of those represented on the painting at any one time.

By the publicity of the assassination it was soon known throughout the city, and thousands crowded the avenues leading to the house where the President lay.

The news of this tragic event flashed with the speed of lightning throughout the land. From Maine to California consternation reigned, and feelings of surprise and grief were depicted on every face. The great man now martyred had for more than four years held the highest place in the gift of the American people, and on him their hopes had centered. The designer of the painting of

"THE LAST HOURS OF LINCOLN,"

JNO. B. BACHELDER, arrived in Washington on the night of his death, and being impressed with the historic importance of the event, at once determined to collect such materials as should be necessary for an historical picture commemorating that sad scene, and should the demand warrant it, to publishing a steel-plate engraving from it. The design for the painting was soon completed, and arrangements having been made with BRADY & Co., Photographers, as soon as the remains of the President left the city each of the persons represented were visited, and at their convenience were posed and photographed in the position which they now occupy in the painting. It being important that the best possible original should be had for the engraver's use, the design was placed in the hands of ALONZO CHAPEL, Esq., the historical painter, to whose genius the painting is to be credited. Much of its completeness is due to the kindness and attention of the persons represented; as all cheerfully gave their time for frequent sittings, both to the designer and painter.

No expense has been spared to produce a work worthy the scene it represents, and the high encomiums given it by eminent judges is the best proof of the result.

To publish any thing now short of a first-class copy of such a painting would be a breach of confidence to those who have so kindly aided in its production. The proprietor has therefore decided to have this picture engraved in the finest style of line and stipple, the engraved surface of the plate to be 19 x 31 inches; believing that nothing short of a genuine work of art will meet the approval, and secure the patronage of the American people, and to those interested the proprietor can most confidently promise a suitable memento of their departed chief.

The engraving is being executed by H. B. HALL, Jr., Esq., the eminent engraver upon steel.

PRICE OF ENGRAVINGS.—PRINTS, $15.00; PLAIN PROOFS, $35.00; INDIA PROOFS, $60.00; ARTIST'S PROOFS (limited to 200 copies which will be numbered and signed by the artist and engraver), $100.00.

A beautiful engraved and photographic Key to the Engraving, will be presented to the subscribers. It is a complete picture of itself, and may be had in advance by subscribers only.

JOHN B. BACHELDER. PUBLISHER. 59 Beekman Street, New York.

The Last Hours of Lincoln

KEY

1 Pres LINCOLN	13 Gov. OGLESBY	25 Gen TODD	37 Col PELOUSE
2 Mrs LINCOLN	14 Speaker COLFAX	26 ROB' LINCOLN	38 Maj HAY
3 Vice Pres JOHNSON	15 Dr STONE	27 Rev Dr GURLEY	39 Gen. MEIGS
4 Maj RATHBONE	16 Surg Gen BARNES	28 Ass' Sec' FIELD	40 Maj ROCKWELL
5 Mr ARNOLD M C	17 Mrs Sen DIXON	29 Adj' Gen HAYNIE	41 Ex Gov FARWELL
6 P M Gen DENNISON	18 Dr. TODD	30 Maj FRENCH	42 Judge CARTTER
7 Sec' WELLES	19 Asst Surg LEALE	31 Gen AUGER	43 Mr ROLLINS M C
8 Att' Gen SPEED	20 Ass' Surg TAFT	32 Col VINCENT	44 Gen MARSTON M C
9 Dr HALL	21 Ass' Sec' OTTO	33 Gen HALLECK	45 Mrs KINNEY
10 Dr LEIBERMANN	22 Gen FARNSWORTH M C	34 Sec' STANTON	46 Miss KINNEY
11 Sec' USHER	23 Sen SUMNER	35 Col RUTHERFORD	47 Miss HARRIS
12 Sec' Mc COLLOCH	24 Surg CRANE	36 Ass' Sec' ECKERT	

BRIEF SAYINGS OF EMINENT MEN.

SURGEON-GENERAL'S OFFICE,
WASHINGTON CITY, *March* 20, 1867.

Col. J. B. BACHELDER.

SIR:—The picture of "The Last Hours of Lincoln," painted by Alonzo Chappel from your design, presents, with remarkable fidelity, the portraits of those in attendance at various times during the night of April 14, 1865, preserving truthfully the principal features of that most sad event.

Very respectfully yours,

J. K. BARNES, *Surgeon-General U. S. A., Brevet Major-General.*

It is certainly a work of great interest and merit. I have looked upon it with the liveliest satisfaction on account of its singularly graphic delineation of the actual scene as myself beheld it, and also because the likenesses of most of the distinguished persons presented by the painting seem to me to be very accurate and striking. P. D. GURLEY, *Pastor of the N. Y. Ave. Pres. Church.*

I cheerfully bear testimony to the accuracy of the Portraits of the persons present on that melancholy occasion, and especially that of the martyred President.

W. T. OTTO, *Assistant Secretary of the Interior.*

It gives me pleasure to testify to the accuracy with which you have represented the principal features of the scene in question, and to the fidelity of the portraits which you have introduced. You have been especially successful in the likeness of President Lincoln. JOHN HAY,

Brevet Colonel, formerly A. D. C. to President Lincoln.

The truthful likeness of President Lincoln, the fidelity of the portraits of those present on that most mournful night, and the excellent grouping of the figures, render this picture peculiarly valuable in an historical point of view, apart from its merits as a work of art.

C. H. CRANE, *Assistant Surgeon-General U. S. Army.*

Without possessing a critical capacity for judgment, I can say, in all sincerity, that the painting, as a whole, is faithful to the scene of the death-chamber on that eventful night, and impressively truthful in its portraiture. D. K. CARTTER, *Chief-Justice.*

☞ The above gentlemen visited President Lincoln during his last hours, and are represented in the painting.

It is admirable as a picture, and of great value for the fidelity of the portraits.

A. A. HUMPHREYS, *Major-General.*

DEAR SIR:—Permit me to thank you for the enjoyment of the luxury of grief afforded me in the viewing of the great picture commemorating "The Last Hours of Lincoln." It is deserving of great praise. If it has a fault, it is its high coloring. As I have personally known nearly all the forty odd persons who appear in it, I can speak with confidence of the truthfulness of the likenesses.

F. E. SPINNER, *Treasurer United States.*

The majority of the portraits could hardly be improved.

O. O. HOWARD, *Major-General.*

I know personally a large majority of the persons represented, and take pleasure in bearing my testimony to the singular fidelity of their portraits. IRA HARRIS, *United States Senator.*

EXTRACT FROM A CRITICISM.

[From the Washington Sunday Herald.]

WASHINGTON, *March* 31, 1867.

A great picture has been designed of the "Last Hours of Abraham Lincoln." The designer is Mr. John B. Bachelder, the painter Alonzo Chappel. * * The value of such a picture of such a scene is enormous, and of a kind to ever increase with time, * * Looking like himself from his finger-nails to his hard, protruding lip, Stanton, with paper and pencil in hand, and uplifted forefinger, is giving instructions to the soldierly General Auger, the then Military Commander of the District, * * Portraits so minutely like I have never seen, even from the brush of Elliot. * * *

The grandeur in the face of Lincoln, is grand indeed. The cold hues of death are warmed to the eye by the red rays of a candle held over him, and the flickering flare causing a Rembrandt-like effect, is very felicitously managed. The eye rests in love and pity on it, turning from those around impatiently. * * *

McCulloch who turns from the scene, and Johnson who sits in the left foreground, are wonderfully like. As is the erect Dennison beyond them; and Meigs, with his hand resting on the door-post, where he stood to prevent disturbing entrances; Dr. Stone and Surgeon-General Barnes, General Todd, Judge Otto, Sumner, Farnsworth, Speaker Colfax, and Governor Oglesby, are looking down on the face of Lincoln with an expression of respectful concern. * * * Judge Cartter and Ex-Governor Farwell stand in front of Meigs, forming the right foreground of the picture; they are given in profile and seem conversing.

The greatness of the picture lies in its correct transcription of an actual scene and perfect portraiture of American men. It is just such a work as, above all others, should be American property, for if ever there was a *National* picture, this is one. ABC.

Sketch of the Life of Abraham Lincoln.

PRICE.

People's Edition. 8vo. Steel Portrait. Cloth $1.50

A Fine Edition. 8vo. Proof Portrait. Fine binding,
beveled boards, Levant cloth, gilt edges................ 3.00

Memorial Edition. On heavy toned paper, large margin.
India Proof Portrait. Morocco, Antique, gilt edges.... 7.00

I am prepared to supply the Trade with the

"SKETCH of the LIFE of ABRAHAM LINCOLN," and the " PORTRAIT of LINCOLN,"

ON LIBERAL TERMS.

My other publications are sold exclusively by Subscription, including

The Steel Engraving of

"The Last Hours of Lincoln;"

The Isometrical Drawing of

"The Gettysburg Battle-field;"

"The History of the Battle of Gettysburg."

The Steel Engraving of

"The Battle of Gettysburg;" (Longstreet's Repulse.)

And the Steel Engravings of the Different

"Episodes of the Battle of Gettysburg."

Each of the latter forming a fine business opportunity for a man of energy, who has a small amount of capital, which he would invest with a certainty of *liberal returns.*

To Canvassers of Experience, having the Capital and Business Capacity to manage the canvass of States, Counties, or Cities, I can offer superior inducements. (See separate notices of subjects.) Orders received for either of the above at the office of publication.

From my intimate business relations with the best Painters, Designers, Steel Engravers, Wood Engravers, and Lithographers, in this City, I am prepared to receive orders from my patrons, and have them executed under my immediate superintendence, in any style required.

JOHN B. BACHELDER, Publisher,

59 Beekman St., New York.

www.ingramcontent.com/pod-product-compliance
Lightning Source LLC
Chambersburg PA
CBHW032204010726
47493CB00008BA/2817